DINNER AT THE NIGHT LIBRARY

DINNER AT THE NIGHT LIBRARY

A NOVEL

HIKA HARADA

TRANSLATED BY PHILIP GABRIEL

HANOVER SQUARE PRESS

HANOVER SQUARE PRESS™

Recycling programs for this product may not exist in your area.

ISBN-13: 978-1-335-01340-8

Dinner at the Night Library

Copyright © 2023 by Hika Harada

First English-language edition published in Great Britain in 2025 by Scribner, an imprint of Simon & Schuster UK. This edition published in 2025.

Originally published in Japan in 2023 as 図書館のお夜食 by Poplar Publishing Co., Ltd.

Translation from the Japanese copyright © 2025 by Philip Gabriel

English language translation rights arranged with Poplar Publishing Co., Ltd.

All rights reserved. No part of this book may be used or reproduced in any manner whatsoever without written permission.

Without limiting the exclusive rights of any author, contributor or the publisher of this publication, any unauthorized use of this publication to train generative artificial intelligence (AI) technologies is expressly prohibited. Harlequin also exercises their rights under Article 4(3) of the Digital Single Market Directive 2019/790 and expressly reserves this publication from the text and data mining exception.

This is a work of fiction. Names, characters, places, and incidents are either the product of the author's imagination or are used fictitiously. Any resemblance to actual persons, living or dead, businesses, companies, events or locales is entirely coincidental.

TM and ® are trademarks of Harlequin Enterprises ULC.

Hanover Square Press
22 Adelaide St. West, 41st Floor
Toronto, Ontario M5H 4E3, Canada
HanoverSqPress.com

HarperCollins Publishers
Macken House, 39/40 Mayor Street Upper
Dublin 1, D01 C9W8, Ireland
www.HarperCollins.com

Printed in U.S.A.

DINNER AT THE NIGHT LIBRARY

EPISODE ONE

SHIROBANBA CURRY

As Otoha Higuchi gave her name to the man in front of the library, she felt a complex mix of feelings—relieved, but at the same time a bit deflated.

People who heard the name Otoha, and her last name, would invariably react by asking, "*Otoha Higuchi?* Were you named after Ichiyo Higuchi?" referring to the famous female writer from the Meiji period, the *ha* in Otoha being written with the same character as the *yo* in Ichiyo, meaning *leaf*. And those who loved books would go on to ask, "What's your favorite story by her?"

But the man here simply said, "Nice to meet you. I'm Yuzuru Sasai. Let me show you around the library," and quickly turned on his heels, walking on ahead.

His height was about five foot seven, slim, and

though somewhat plain looking, had a nicely shaped nose. Otoha, just over five feet tall, only came up to his shoulders. Some might see him as good-looking, others a bit too ordinary. It was that sort of face.

Yet he wasn't as curt as his looks and opening words might suggest, and noticing the wheeled suitcase Otoha was pulling, he reached out and offered, "Let me help you with that."

"I'm good," she said. "There's a trick to pulling it. One of the wheels is about to come off, and you have to favor the other one . . ."

His face lit up.

"Like *Anne of Green Gables*?"

"Huh?" she said reflexively, and he smiled sheepishly before settling back into his usual expression.

"Pardon me," he said. "You can leave your bag inside, at the reception desk, if that's alright."

"Sure."

"I understand you came all the way from Tohoku?"

"I did."

"You must be tired. I'll tell you about the library a little today, introduce you to the staff, and then show you to the dorm."

"No, I'm fine, and ready to work," Otoha replied.

After seeing off the movers in the morning, she'd taken a train straight to Tokyo carrying her suitcase and one other bag. The email she'd received had a Google map attached, but it had taken her far longer than she'd expected to find this place, roughly described in the email as being *in a Tokyo suburb*. Happily, though, she'd managed to make it by 7:00 p.m., the appointed time.

Resigning from her previous job, getting a sudden new offer, changing jobs, moving. . . It had all happened within a month and she was, frankly, worn out. But this was her first day on a new job, and it was one that dealt with books, her dream, one she'd almost lost once, so she wanted to be seen as a solid, eager worker.

Past the automatic doors, the entrance walls were a whitish marble inset with a small plaque, which hung at about eye level for Otoha.

"This is all real marble here," Sasai explained.

"Wow. That's amazing."

The small square plaque was only about three inches on one side. Inside was a butterfly the size of the tip of a thumb. She'd never seen that kind before, and found herself drawing closer to examine it. "A butterfly?" she asked, turning around toward Sasai.

"Actually, it's a moth."

Otoha yelped. "Isn't that sort of a—creepy thing to display?"

She inspected it closely and saw that despite the shiny azure wings, its body was a bit thick for a butterfly.

"It's supposed to be a . . . sort of charm."

"Eh?"

"I heard the owner put it there to ward off evil," Sasai explained, without much interest.

"Can something like that ward off anything?"

"It can, since people who dislike it never go near it again."

"I suppose you're right," Otoha said.

"Really, only people who are interested come to this library. We prefer that casual sightseers—or those who just want to take a quick look—stay away."

"I see."

"And moths are night butterflies. In foreign countries they don't look down on moths the way we do. They just divide them into daytime butterflies and nighttime butterflies."

"I'm not looking down on them . . ." Otoha said. *How could he think I'm the sort who discriminates like that?* she thought, a bit miffed.

Still, Sasai seemed unfazed. "Is that so?"

"Can I meet the owner and say hello today?" Otoha asked, thinking she needed to express her thanks for the job.

"I'm afraid that's impossible."

"Huh?" *I'm here because the owner asked me to be, right?*

"I myself have never even met the owner. Only talked on the phone or email."

EPISODE ONE

"B-but aren't you the manager here, Mr. Sasai?"

"I am."

"Even so?"

"That's right. I don't think any of the staff have ever met the owner."

"Really?"

"The owner is abroad most of the year."

"Is that right?"

"I don't think investigating their identity will lead to anything good."

How come? Otoha was about ask, but before she could Sasai had strode away. His figure seemed to firmly convey a message: no more questions. Otoha trotted off behind him.

Beyond the marbled entrance was another automatic door, and past that, a ticket window on the right and a turnstile on the left. A woman was seated behind the ticket window counter, and there was a sign on the wall listing entrance fees.

Entrance fee: ¥1,000
Monthly passes: ¥10,000
Yearly passes: ¥50,000

Sasai introduced Otoha to the woman.

"This is Ms. Otoha Higuchi. She'll be working with us starting today."

The woman stood up and bowed politely. When she lowered her head, silky long black hair fell from her shoulders. Otoha found her lovely.

"It's very nice to meet you," Otoha hurriedly reciprocated, bowing just as deeply.

"Ms. Higuchi, this is our receptionist, Mai Kitazato."

This Ms. Kitazato said not a word back to her. Expressionless, unsmiling. Perhaps Sasai seemed used to her behavior, as he simply asked, "Could you give Ms. Higuchi a visitor pass?" Mai gave a small nod and handed Otoha a pass on a lanyard. It seemed they'd prepared this in advance for her.

"Tomorrow we'll have a regular staff pass ready for you." Sasai showed her the pass around his neck. "If you press it here you can get in."

The entrance turnstile was simpler and smaller scale than the ones at train stations, and when he held up the pass to it, the turnstile opened. Otoha followed suit.

"Ms. Kitazato might not look it, but she won the national championship in karate."

"What? *Her*?"

"So best not to mess around there."

"My gosh . . ."

"I bet you were just thinking how tight the security is for a library."

Spot on, she wanted to say, but shook her head.

"No, I don't think that."

"And that ¥1,000 is a steep admission fee?"

Again, he'd nailed it. This time she couldn't help but smile faintly and nod.

"A little."

"It's okay. Everybody says that," Sasai murmured as he went into the library.

"In the past we let everyone in for free," he went on. "But we had things stolen, and some people were unreasonable and complained, saying things like 'Why just *old* books? Why don't you have any books I wanna read?' So the owner decided to start charging admission. It's more to keep out the oddballs than to earn money."

"I see."

"As I've said several times, we'd just like the people who want to come here to come."

"I get that."

"But even after we started charging admission, we've had people stealing books. So there's an alarm that goes off in the library if someone tries to take a book without permission."

"That *is* pretty strict."

"The books here are all precious ones, found nowhere else. So please keep that in mind."

"Understood. That's very clear."

They went through the second automatic glass door, finally entering the library.

Otoha gulped and looked upward.

At the entrance the ceiling rose up to the second floor, with bookshelves reaching to the ceiling, crammed full of books.

"This is amazing! It's so beautiful."

And it was a magnificent sight, books rising all the way to the vaulted ceiling. Yet on the outside, the library was an unassuming neat gray structure, so the contrast was indeed striking.

"It is rather nice, isn't it." Sasai was cool and collected, unlike the excited Otoha.

"It's amazing—almost the very library I've been dreaming of forever," Otoha said.

"Glad to hear it."

Once again Sasai strode off inside.

She wanted to take a closer look at the books lined up there, but still found herself trotting off to keep up with him.

Past the room with the vaulted ceilings, they entered a spacious area. At the entrance was another reception desk, behind which were seated a man and woman who seemed to be library staff. Both were in casual clothes with a black apron. When they saw Sasai and Otoha they rose to their feet. The woman was about the same height as Otoha, the man quite tall, about five foot nine, and solidly built.

"This is Ms. Otoha Higuchi, who's come here today to work with us," Sasai explained.

EPISODE ONE

"I'm Naoto Tokai," the man said.

"And my name's Minami Enokida," said the woman.

Unlike Sasai and Mai, these two were smiling. At long last Otoha felt reassured. She'd been asking herself what she should do if the entire staff turned out to be like them, attractive, yet cool and detached. She was happy, too, that, though a little older, they were of her same generation.

"Otoha Higuchi—almost the same characters as the author Ichiyo Higuchi's name, right? Is there some connection?" Minami asked, smiling broadly. Otoha had been asked this so many times she was tired of it, yet now the familiar question brought only a sigh of relief.

"Yes, my mother is a big fan of Ichiyo Higuchi, and when she married and her last name changed to Higuchi she decided she wanted to name her daughter using the character *yo*, or *ha* meaning *leaf*."

"Got it. So—do you read a lot of Ichiyo Higuchi's work?"

"I have read it, yes. My favorite is 'The Thirteenth Night.'"

"That's a very short one, but heartrending, isn't it. The woman in the story—"

Totally ignoring their conversation, Sasai interrupted. "For the time being," he said, "we'll be having Ms. Higuchi processing books."

"I see." Tokai nodded. "It's tough work, so good luck."

"We'll stop by later to give you a hand," Minami said.

The two of them seemed to feel for her. Tokai smiled wanly, while Minami looked sympathetic.

"Is the work that difficult?" Otoha was a bit worried.

The two of them looked at each other, and Otoha noticed something: they almost looked like twins. Not their faces so much as their gestures and expressions, the whole vibe that surrounded them.

"It's not so hard, but kind of repetitive, so you can get tired of it," Tokai said.

"I don't particularly mind it. And it's something all new staff need to learn," Minami added.

"Sorry about that, but we'll help you out," they both piped in. Despite these warnings, the two of them seemed upbeat, and the tension drained out of Otoha a bit.

"Later on, let's eat the staff dinner together. Tonight's menu is shirobanba, as I recall."

Shirobanba? What could that *be?* Otoha wondered, but Sasai had once again strode off and she had to hurry to catch up. She glanced around and saw the two of them, Tokai and Minami, right hands both raised, waving farewell. Instinctively she waved back.

"Come this way," Sasai said and walked off quickly, noiselessly.

The next room—and the next one after that—all

had identical bookshelves along the walls, each packed full of books, and within the larger rooms, bookshelves in the middle as well.

After passing through most of the library, they arrived at the last room, one with no visible exit.

Meaning they had arrived at the very end of the first floor.

Yet Sasai walked to the very back of the room . . . toward the bookshelves, in other words, and came to a halt in front of them.

"It's behind this. Where your first job is," he explained.

"Huh? But you can't go any farther," Otoha exclaimed.

"Not true. It's behind here."

When she didn't seem to get it, Sasai made a wide gesture with his arms.

"*Open up, door!*" he intoned.

What the heck is he up to? A grown man acting like a child! . . . She looked back and forth between him and the bookshelf, thoroughly perplexed.

And sure enough the bookshelves began to clatter open, left and right.

And there really was a room behind them.

"You gotta be kidding me," Otoha murmured.

The only time she'd ever seen anything like this was in foreign dramas where rich people had safe rooms.

". . . You were just thinking how childish I am, weren't you," Sasai said.

Otoha no longer had the strength to deny it. She nodded weakly.

"At least I didn't say *Open sesame*. You should give me that much."

He smiled broadly for the very first time.

PREVIOUSLY, OTOHA HAD BEEN working in a bookstore in a train terminal building in the far-off northern Tohoku area.

I want to have a job that involves books . . . that had been her longtime dream. In college she'd majored in Japanese literature and had even written a paper on the author Osamu Dazai for a modern Japanese literature seminar. She obtained certificates to teach Japanese in schools, as well as calligraphy. She wanted to qualify to be a librarian, too, but couldn't manage it after moving from the countryside to live by herself in the city. She hadn't taken out any student loans, but she knew her parents were sending her support from their meager resources, so she took on a part-time job to help make ends meet.

After she failed to pass the teacher's employment exam in her hometown, she tried to find a job involving books—at publishers, book distributors, chain bookstores—any place she could think of, but nothing panned out. She was offered a job at a manufacturing company her college had introduced her to, and passed, but she was dying to work with books, even if it was a part-time job, so she turned down the company's job offer. She went back to her hometown and became a contract employee at a bookstore.

Her parents were concerned. "You managed to go to a college in Tokyo, so shouldn't you work for a large company at least once? New graduates have only one chance to get a good job. How is this job at a bookstore any different from a part-time one?"

"I want to do work I like," she parried when she began the job. "Don't worry, of course I'm going to keep on looking for something permanent too!"

At the interview at the bookstore, she ardently declared that she *Loved novels!* and happily was assigned to the literature section of the bookstore.

She enjoyed working at a bookstore in a station terminal building, though gradually the job made her exhausted, physically and mentally. Working overtime was a given, as was the paltry salary. But more than that, she and the mid-forties male manager didn't get along at all. He'd been sent from the bookstore's headquarters, and from the start he liked to categorize the staff members into two groups, as either *cheerful* or *gloomy*, and this odd way of thinking led him to only speak directly with those whom he found *cheerful*.

For better or worse, Otoha fell into his *cheerful* category. "You have such a bright smile, Ms. Higuchi," he commented. All well and good, but it became a burden, with the manager often saying, "Cheerful Ms. Higuchi can do it," assigning her time-consuming jobs, and larger tasks to do. She was afraid if she were seen as *gloomy* she'd lose her job, so she forced herself to act as bright and upbeat as she could despite all the extra work.

Customers often had ridiculous complaints, but when they did, the manager shoved them onto Otoha to deal with. For a job she should be enjoying, her dissatisfaction grew by the day.

Low sales also forced a reduction in shelf space for literature and Otoha had a run-in with the head office about it. When she reported the head office's request to the manager, his reaction was "You're being so gloomy, Ms. Higuchi. That's not like you!"

After this, she decided she didn't want to want to work at the store anymore.

From that day on he never spoke to her. Another incident also happened that she was involved in, making it even harder to continue working there.

The manager, of course, did nothing to back her up.

Ever since she started the job, she'd been posting anonymous messages on social media as a bookstore employee. At first, they were full of her hopes for the job, but before long she found herself using it as a forum to air her complaints and troubles. Around the time she was thinking of quitting, she received a DM from someone who'd read her posts.

> Hello. I've been reading your Tweets. My handle is Seven Rainbows. I always can feel how much you love books, especially novels. I understand you're thinking of changing jobs. I'm sorry to hear that. If you don't mind, I may be able to introduce you to another job dealing with books. I wonder if you'd be interested.

Her honest reaction was a mix of happiness and suspicion.

Of course, she'd be happy if she could continue working with books. That went without saying. Yet the whole thing sounded sketchy. Very much so.

Before long, though, another DM arrived.

> I run a small library on the outskirts of Tokyo. The library doesn't have a set name. If you need to refer to it, please call it The Night Library. Actually, it's open only at night, from 7 to 12 a.m. The workday is from 4 p.m. to 1 a.m., with a one-hour break included.

> Our holdings don't include books found in ordinary libraries. Instead our books are all those from the personal collections of deceased writers, which are

donated to us after their passing, and our main work is to display them and organize them. Patrons are allowed to view these, but as a rule we don't lend any out. We call ourselves a library but in actual fact we're more like a book museum.

We can't pay much in salary, only about ¥150,000 a month take-home pay, but there's a dorm behind the library, admittedly a bit ramshackle, and you can live there for free. Utilities you'd pay for yourself, but Wi-Fi is free. And the building has AC and gas stoves. If you'd like to see it, I can send you a floor plan.

As she read this, Otoha felt like pinching herself.
The pay was, indeed, low, but the other conditions weren't bad. It might be in the suburbs of Tokyo, but it still made her happy that she might be able to live there.
But what attracted her the most was the notion of dealing with writers' own personal collections. These were the books not just written by the author themselves, but all the books that an author owned and might've read throughout their lifetime, books that might've inspired that author's own love for reading.

If you're interested, please get in touch.

She was bewildered, unsure what to do, but went ahead and replied. A reply came back immediately with a Zoom link and a time for an online interview.

The other thing that surprised her was that the Zoom interview was audio only, with the interviewer's voice filtered through a voice changer. Throughout the interview the other person, calling himself or herself the owner, sounded like an older man involved in some dodgy kidnapping scheme.

But what kept her from giving up on the job were the glimpses, behind the weird voice, of the speaker's obvious affection for literature.

"Please talk to me about books," the owner asked.

"Books . . ."

"What you read as a child, the books you've encountered since, what books you're reading at present. Those sorts of things."

"Well, how much should I say? This might get pretty long."

"I don't mind at all. Tell me everything. From the very beginning. Like you're talking about everything you've ever read."

This threw Otoha for a moment. But this person with the weird, muffled voice was a wonderful listener. The owner listened to her intently, reacting warmly at times to what Otoha had to say. This person must be quite erudite, Otoha thought as they spoke. *I've never enjoyed talking with anyone this much, or learned so much!* The owner had read almost all the books Otoha mentioned, and when Otoha mentioned a new one said, "Just a moment, I'd like to read that one too," and apparently jotted down the title. *What a sincere person*, Otoha thought. *When they don't know something they honestly admit it.*

Otoha was growing fond of this owner and was sure she wanted to work under them.

Over three hours went by in a flash.

". . . You passed," the owner said.

"Excuse me?"

"I'd love for you to come work at our library, Ms. Higuchi . . . If you're alright with it, that is."

Otoha felt, for the very first time, that the world accepted her.

The owner had never asked her why she'd left her job at the bookstore, and Otoha felt relieved she didn't have to explain the reason.

BEHIND THE BOOKSHELVES LAY a slumbering cave.

Or at least that's the feeling Otoha got from the unadorned room with its walls painted black.

Cardboard boxes lay stacked up along the sides, with three desks lined up in a U shape, a computer on top of each. Two older women stood in front of these.

Like the others they both wore black aprons. One woman was heavyset, and had on a long dark red dress with a fine flower pattern. The other woman was slim and wore camouflage-patterned shirt and trousers. In places where there weren't cardboard boxes at their feet, there were stacks of books up to the two women's ankles.

"This is . . .?" Otoha ventured.

"As I mentioned, it's the section where collections are processed," Sasai said. "You can call it the collections processing room."

"I see."

"And these are Ako and Masako."

The two women bowed deeply.

"I'm Ako."

"I'm Masako."

The one in the dress was Ako, the one in the shirt, Masako.

"I'm Otoha Higuchi. Very nice to meet you."

Otoha bowed deeply too.

"My, you're so polite."

"So this is the young lady?"

Ako and Masako's words overlapped.

"Newly hired people learn the ropes by working here first," Sasai said. "Collection processing is, you could say, the heart, or maybe the brain, of the library . . . Anyway, it's the most important place. You could say that the entire library rests on these two women's shoulders."

Sasai said this solemnly, and Ako and Masako exchanged a look and chuckled.

"We don't know about that."

"You're making us blush."

Sasai bowed to them and said, "I leave Ms. Higuchi in your hands," and left the room. On the way out he didn't say *Open, door!* but the door opened automatically anyway.

Otoha blankly watched him leave as Ako said, "Ms. Higuchi," in a calm voice. "Did you just arrive here today?"

"That's right."

"Then you must be tired."

Before she could say "Not at all," Masako interjected with a "She's young, and healthy, after all. Don't lump her together with the likes of us!"

Somehow, both women's words fit how Otoha was feeling. She was tired, true enough, yet it was also true that she could push herself a little more. So she left her response vague, a smile somehow plastered on her face as she looked at each of them in turn.

"Well okay, then." Masako smirked wryly as she looked at Otoha.

"Anyway, we'll give you a quick summary of what the work involves and have you try it with us."

"Sure, thank you!" Otoha said.

Ako took a black apron out of a locker in a corner of the room.

"This is our uniform, you might say," Ako said. "Work clothes. You can wear whatever you like but when you're working keep this apron on over it. Only the manager, Mr. Sasai, doesn't wear one, except when he's behind the reception desk."

"Well, he also goes out to meet people," Masako added. "The aprons are convenient, though, and keep your clothes from getting dirty."

"That's right."

"Black's a bit subdued but it goes with any kind of clothes, and when we meet with the surviving family members it comes across as formal, without having to wear proper mourning dress."

I see, Otoha thought. *So that's why they chose black.*

"Regular size should be okay I would think."

"Yes. That would be fine," Otoha said.

Otoha took the apron Ako handed her and put it on. The apron was a bit oversized, and even after adjusting the tie around her neck it was a little baggy.

Otoha glanced at the women and noticed that both of their aprons fit perfectly. Ako was heavyset but hers didn't look overly tight, while Masako was so thin her nickname might well be The Wire, and yet the material didn't hang loosely at all.

As Otoha looked back and forth between the two, Masako chuckled. "Ah, so you noticed. We're the only two who had our aprons form fitted. Ako's good with her hands and with sewing, so she took them in and let them out as needed so they'd fit us better."

Ako chuckled too.

"Young people can wear clothes that are a bit too big or too small and still look attractive, but for much older folks if they don't fit just right it looks ugly."

"Cool."

Oops, wrong word. Otoha's hands flew to her mouth in embarrassment. She shouldn't be this informal with older people.

"We'll take yours in, too, sometime to make it fit better."

"Are you—sure?" Otoha asked.

"Sooner or later."

"Shall we get to it then?" Masako said firmly.

"Okay!"

"I'm sure you've heard about the library from the owner?"

Ako opened a cardboard box at her feet.

"Some of it, yes," Otoha said.

"To review, this library takes the collections of writers—mainly novelists—after they've passed, to preserve them and put some of the books on display. Not just books those writers wrote themselves, but all the books they ever owned, read, and collected in their lifetime."

"Yes, I was told that."

"Some writers themselves will leave their collections to us, or donate them while they're still alive as they organize their books. In other cases after the writer has passed, their families aren't sure what to do with their collections and leave them with us."

Masako took over from Ako. "At any rate, we're sent a large amount of books every month, which are first gathered in this room, where it's our job to organize them."

"I see."

"In actual fact, though, we have way too many books," Masako said, arms folded, "and we are storing those of recently deceased writers in an offsite storehouse."

"Oh . . ."

Masako picked up a seal from the top of a desk and showed it to Otoha.

"This is what we call a collection seal. We stamp this in the inside back cover of all the books. Some of these stamps are also ones that writers chose while they were still living, while we make other stamps after consulting with their families after they've passed. Generally, we make seals we think the writers will like, with the rule, though, being that they include the writer's full name so you can tell at a glance whose book it is. Otherwise, it could lead to trouble later on.

"At first it was more haphazard, freer, with, for instance, an author's first name only below an illustration, and ones written in cursive that was hard to read, all sorts of variations. I mean *we* always know whose are whose, though.

"What I'm saying is that this process is very important, so make sure to stamp them precisely. Today, why don't we start by having you do this task for us."

"Alright," Otoha said.

That's it? Stamping books? Though relieved, Otoha couldn't help feeling a bit let down as well.

"Mmm?" Masako said, as if reading Otoha's expression. "This *is* a critical part of the work, you know."

"It's okay, I don't mind," Otoha said.

"And it's not as easy as it looks," Ako said.

Otoha took a seat at the desk and began stamping books. And sure enough, until you got the hang of it, it was harder than she'd thought.

You needed to make sure the hard wood seal had enough ink, evenly distributed, otherwise it wouldn't come out right. The two women were gentle in their directions except when it came to making sure she stamped cleanly and straight—this was nonnegotiable. And if you shut the book right way after stamping it the seal smudged on the facing page. The first few times Otoha tried it, the women hovered close, supervising. After stamping a book, you needed to insert a special sheet of blotting paper.

It took more strength to press down evenly than Otoha had imagined. And it indeed was tiring.

"Keep on stamping, and I'll explain the process more," Masako said as she saw Otoha was getting the knack of it.

"Okay."

"The books that are stamped are inputted into a databank. The title, author's name, the edition, the year of publication are all inputted. And you need to glance through each volume and note down if it contains any handwritten marginal notes. This is all preserved online, but only on the intranet, in-house, since our policy is for books to not leave the library. If other people want to see the materials and information they have to come here."

"I understand."

"After we've organized an author's collection, we keep the information not only in digital form, but in a book devoted to each author."

"Really?"

"Like this."

Masako took out a book and showed her. A simple dark red volume with the name *Taeko Nagamine* written in gold lettering on the cover. An author Otoha had never read. She had the feeling, though, that she'd seen an article on the author's passing sometime last year. A writer who'd debuted in her teens but hadn't published anything in quite some years.

"These books are shelved on the second floor. Each and every volume nicely bound."

"That's amazing."

"It's the least we can do when they're kind enough to donate their collections to us."

"Some authors owned a massive number of books, while for some they had barely enough to fill a single volume."

Ako laughed.

"Those types are in the minority, though."

"Nowadays with the rise of digital books, print books are decreasing, so I imagine dealing with e-books the author owned will become an issue."

"I would think so." Otoha nodded, her hands never resting.

"The books that have been processed, whose data have been recorded, are divided into those we put onto the shelves outside or those we keep in the stacks inside. We don't want to have multiple copies of the same book on the shelves, so the books of some authors' personal collections that duplicate our existing holdings are stored in the stacks."

"If you do that, then don't you end up with dozens of copies of the donated book?"

"We do."

Masako pursed her lips.

"Which is both an important point, but a headache, too. We get a lot of precious old volumes and out-of-print books, but recently we received many books that have only just been published, with the owner telling us we have to save them all."

"I see."

"The owner said it's because for the author and his family, for fans and researchers, each and every book that passed through the author's hands is one of a kind."

"I can understand that."

"The owner apparently said we should treat all the books like they're lovers of ours who've passed away. But even we if put them in storage, there's a limit to how much can fit."

"That makes sense," Otoha said.

"Someday it will be all full. And then what do we do? . . . I think the only thing will be to get rid of them."

"But the owner does have a point, maybe two or three, actually," Ako said, rolling her eyes. "The day might come when a deceased author becomes really popular, right? Like one of the books is made into a film, wins a film prize, and get noticed worldwide, or maybe wins some other kind of prize. Then this place will be packed."

"It's hard to know these days why certain things take off. Famous people's social media, for instance, or TV shows," Otoha said, nodding deeply. When she'd worked at the bookstore she'd seen this occur.

"But that kind of thing happens very, very rarely . . . Like, at a rate of one in hundreds of thousands. Easier to win the lottery," Masako said, dismissing the idea. "And also for fans and researchers, every book owned by a writer is precious. A notation in the margins or a single turned down corner of a page could be a step forward in their research."

"Ah, so Ako-san, were you by chance a Japanese literature major?"

"I was! How did you know?" Ako asked.

"Because that's the way people in Japanese literature departments who've written a research paper think."

"I guess—you did that, too?"

"That's right!" Otoha exclaimed.

Otoha and Ako instinctively slapped a pair of high fives, Masako looking on and smiling wryly again.

"Well, there is a higher probability of these books being useful to a researcher than them winning a film prize," Masako said, reluctantly admitting the point.

After 10:00 p.m., Minami Enokida came in from the second-floor reception desk.

"Good job, everyone," she said.

"You too," Ako replied.

"I've come to take Otoha to get something to eat."

"Right. It's been three hours, so about time to take a break," Masako said, glancing up at the clock on the wall. She then turned to Otoha. "Why don't you go have the staff dinner now?"

"Oh—okay, but . . ."

Was it really okay to leave these senior staff members to carry on working and take a break by herself?

"I brought my own bento, so I'll eat here when it's the right time," Ako said.

"And I'll go to eat when everyone else is finished. I want to eat by myself," Masako said.

The two women were clear on this. When it came to meals, they seemed set in their ways.

"And you can leave after you eat."

"Alright, but . . ." Otoha hesitated.

She'd heard from Mr. Sasai that the library was open from 7:00 p.m. to midnight, and that the work schedule was from 4:00 p.m. to 1:00 a.m., with a one-hour break.

"You're not used to the work yet, Otoha, and you've just come all the way from Tohoku. You should go home and rest up. You need to unpack, too, I imagine."

"You should." Ako nodded.

Otoha was a bit tense now, so she didn't feel tired, but she knew that if she went back to her room she'd probably collapse.

"Are you sure . . .?" she asked.

Was it really alright? She glanced at Minami, who was smiling broadly and nodding. Ako and Masako's expressions told her Minami's smile was genuine.

Otoha had long been sensitive to people's expressions at her workplace. They might tell her to "Go ahead and take a break," but when she did, her colleagues gossiped behind her back: *What an inconsiderate person. Doesn't she know we're suggesting that just to be polite? Usually people would tell the more senior staff to take a break first, wouldn't they?* So she was perpetually doubtful if what others told her reflected their true feelings.

"Of course. Go right ahead," Masako said, nodding deeply.

"Then I guess I'll do that . . . but if it's okay . . ." Otoha had just thought of something. "Would it be possible for me to sit at the reception desk? . . . Just a little . . . just for a little while is fine, really. I'd like to get a feel for the library."

Otoha suggested this hesitantly, but Minami assented right away. "Of course, that would be fine. The timing's just right. After we eat, I'm taking over from Mr. Tokai there, who you met alongside me earlier, so let's go sit together."

"Talk about motivated," Masako said, commending her. "But don't overdo it the first day so you don't regret it later on."

"I won't. Well, I'll be going then," Otoha said.

As she and Minami exited the room, she couldn't help glancing back at the space between bookshelves they'd passed through.

"Uh . . .?" Otoha began.

"Yes?"

"How does this entrance and exit work? A little while ago Mr. Sasai said *Open up, door!* and it opened. Does it really open like that, like magic?"

"Really? Mr. Sasai did that?" Minami burst out laughing. "Imagine—so even he does things like that. No, it's not like that. Look over there."

Minami walked back over to the bookshelves and fluttered her hand in front of them. And the bookshelves again slid smoothly apart.

Ako and Masako, inside the room, looked up at them in surprise.

"Sorry. I'm showing Otoha how the door opens."

"Goodness. Is that what you're up to?" the women inside said.

"See, there's a sensor up at the top," Minami explained. "If you wave your hand like this or let it touch your body, it'll open."

"But Mr. Sasai . . ."

"I'm sure that when he said *Open up, door!* he touched the sensor."

Minami turned and walked off toward the second floor.

"Mr. Sasai's more playful than he seems," Otoha said.

"That's a first, believe me. I'm going to tease him about it."

"Please don't tell him I told you."

"I won't, but I'm sure it won't take long for him to figure it out."

"You think?"

"No worries. He doesn't look happy or laugh much, but by the same token he doesn't get angry or sad either."

Is that how it is? Puzzled over this, Otoha trotted after her.

"What happens if a patron touches the sensor?" she asked.

"It'll open up. They're all pretty surprised by it."

"Is it okay for that to happen?"

"Well, it only happens a couple of times a year," Minami said.

The dining hall was in one corner on the second floor. At the entrance was a wooden sign that said *Library Cafe*.

The name was a little old-fashioned, or maybe a bit too direct, but inside was, indeed, set up like a simple cafe. On the floor were tables and chairs made of light-colored, natural wood. Several people were enjoying coffee or a light meal, or reading a book.

At the entrance was an old-fashioned ticket-vending machine and several posted menus. Otoha wanted to study them, but Minami strode right past them, so she gave up and followed her in. Minami took a seat at a six-person table in the farthest corner.

"If we come here, you're bound to see other library staff," she said.

"Is that right?"

"Because everyone has pretty much the same break time . . . apart from people at the reception desk."

Just then, an older man approached.

"You're both good with the set dinner?" he asked.

"Yes, we are!" Minami answered eagerly. "Thank you as always, Mr. Kinoshita."

"Right," he replied and gave a short nod.

"This is Ms. Otoha Higuchi, who just started today."

"Hello. It's very nice to meet you." Otoha stood and bowed.

"Nice to meet you as well," Mr. Kinoshita said lightly. "Would you like some iced coffee after you eat?"

Iced coffee—in the winter? Otoha had her doubts, but Minami whispered to her, "Mr. Kinoshita's iced coffee is absolutely delicious," and Otoha nodded.

Kinoshita seemed another example of a person who was a bit curt, but kind.

"Before he came here, Mr. Kinoshita was a barista at a famous coffee shop in Ginza," Minami told her as she watched his retreating figure.

"For real?"

"He was sort of the symbol of that coffee shop, but he and the owner had some minor falling out and he was let go. The customers were taken aback by this since they'd always figured he was the owner or manager. That's how popular he was."

"Is that right? Did you hear all this from Mr. Kinoshita?"

She asked this since Mr. Kinoshita didn't seem like the type to go on and on about his past.

"No, not really. He doesn't talk about that. Mr. Tokai loves coffee, and he said he'd visited that shop in Ginza a number of times. But among coffee afficionados it's a well-known story and apparently all over the internet."

"What happened to the coffee shop?" Otoha asked.

"It lost customers for a while, but it's in a prime location in Ginza. They put in a coffee machine and lowered the prices a little and their customer base has changed from before. I hear it's doing well again. Some of them apparently think the coffee they have there is still made by Mr. Kinoshita."

That's terrible, Otoha thought, but knew it wasn't so unusual.

As they were talking Mr. Kinoshita returned and placed a tray of plates on the table.

"Wow," Otoha couldn't help saying.

On the tray were two plates of a yellowish curry.

"Today's menu is *shirobanba*. Monday is *shirobanba* day."

"Curry always perks me up."

Minami nodded.

"What do you mean by *shirobanba*?" Otoha asked.

"You don't know?" Kinoshita asked. "You haven't read it? It's from Yasushi Inoue's novel *Shirobanba*. It's a re-creation of the curry an old woman in the story cooks. Shirobanba, by the way, are the so-called snow bugs, teeny tiny insects that have a white puff on their wings that looks like cotton. They look like little flakes of snow."

"I haven't read it. Sorry."

Kinoshita said, "I only read it after I came here, so who am I to brag? But it was very interesting."

"I'll be sure to read it right away," Otoha said.

"We must have many copies in our collection," he said. "You should get them to lend you one. If you take good care of it, it'll be okay."

"I'll do that," Otoha said.

"Well, let's eat."

"Go ahead. Enjoy," Kinoshita said and left.

Otoha picked up her spoon and took a bite. It was typical curry and tasted good. At first it seemed mild, but then it got spicier, with a unique aroma. *I could really get to like this*, she thought.

"It's good, isn't it?" Minami whispered.

"Sure is."

The carrots and onions cut in small cubes she recognized, but there was another vegetable, likewise stewed to translucency, she didn't. When she tasted it, it felt like it would easily fall apart.

"What is this?" Otoha asked. "This vegetable is so soft and fresh . . ."

She'd never seen this sort of vegetable in curry before.

"That's daikon radish."

"Seriously? Daikon?"

Daikon in curry—now that was a first. It worked, surprisingly.

"When Mr. Kinoshita was scouted for this job, the owner made it a condition that he re-create and serve several recipes from novels and essays the owner chose. Since Mr. Kinoshita's an excellent cook as well as barista."

"What else is in this?" Otoha asked. "It's savory, as if there's meat, but I don't see any."

The small cubes of vegetables were front and center, with torn-off scraps of some kind of meat hidden beneath. But this, too, must lend the curry its unique flavor. She raised her spoon and stared at it intently. "Ah—!"

"You get it?"

"It's corned beef!" Otoha exclaimed.

"Excellent. If you read *Shirobanba* you'll find even more details. The meals here change each day of the week. Monday is *shirobanba*. The meals are only ¥300, including coffee. With the chef from a famous shop in Ginza."

"No kidding, it's the best."

As they ate the curry, a middle-aged man came over.

"Hello, my name's Tokuda. A pleasure to meet you." He was a chubby man, wearing round glasses.

"Mr. Tokuda also used to work in a bookstore," Minami explained. "He joined us about six months ago."

"I'm Otoha Higuchi."

In a rush of words, Tokuda said, "I'm ten years older than Mr. Sasai, just an ordinary, low-level employee, while he's the manager. After I got sick and quit the bookstore I worked at, I took some time off, so I started here only recently. The owner, too, told me to take it easy."

"I see. It's nice to meet you," Otoha said.

Tokuda ordered the dinner from Mr. Kinoshita and went off to get a glass of water.

"Mr. Tokuda's a nice man," Minami murmured, "but a bit high-strung, you could say, when it comes to questions of seniority at work . . . It bothers him that Mr. Sasai is above him here. Other than that, he's very kind, competent, and a decent person. Since he was hired later, I don't think there's a problem that he has a lower rank even though he's older. The staff here are of all ages—take Ako and Masako, for instance."

"I can see that."

"I think he feels good that there's a person like you, younger than him and hired after him."

"I wonder . . ."

Mr. Tokuda came back, a bit fidgety. He brought glasses of water for Otoha and Minami as well.

As she sipped the water, Otoha considered what Minami had said. Other than job titles, Tokuda didn't seem that concerned about anything else. She'd been worrying that it might be hard to work with someone so focused on rank, but here he was, nice enough to bring a glass of water over for a woman considerably younger than him.

Still, she thought it was best to err on the side of politeness when dealing with him.

As advertised, after their meal iced coffee was served. Very aromatic, but not bitter.

"I think that iced coffee is an absolute must after curry," Mr. Kinoshita explained. "Just my idea, though."

"It does go well after curry. It's delicious."

"This is cold-brewed coffee. I've been extracting it since last night."

"Is that right? I've never had it before."

"Cold-brewed coffee?"

"I've heard the name, but had no idea it tasted this good."

I never really had the leisure to sit back and enjoy a nice cup of coffee, Otoha thought. *When I was a college student, or after I started working, I didn't have the money, and if I wanted to chat with friends, a chain coffee shop was plenty fine.*

"This might be the best iced coffee I've ever had," she said.

"Where did you have the second best?"

"Seven Eleven."

Kinoshita burst out laughing.

"That makes it worth brewing even more. Seven Eleven's iced coffee is actually pretty good."

"I never drank it much until I came here. Coffee, that is," Mr. Tokuda said. "I never thought it could be this good."

"Well, men's opinions don't concern me that much," Kinoshita said, overly blunt, and everyone there had a good laugh. Except for Tokuda.

As promised, after their staff dinner, Otoha got her chance to sit at the reception desk.

"Are you really okay?" Minami asked. "If you get tired just say the word."

"Al—alright."

After they'd sat there for a while an elderly lady came in. Her white hair was neatly arranged, and she wore a burgundy-colored coat and had a cane. She wore oversized light-colored sunglasses, and walked rather slowly.

"Good evening," she said, her voice quavering.

"Good evening, Ms. Ninomiya," Minami quickly responded. "It's cold out. Are you alright?"

"Yes. I took a taxi here."

"Shall I call one for you when you leave?"

"Alright. I'll tell you when I'm ready."

As she spoke, Ms. Ninomiya seemed to notice Otoha and turned her gaze to her.

"This is Otoha Higuchi, who just joined us today," Minami explained.

"So very nice to meet you," Otoha said, springing to her feet and bowing deeply.

"My goodness, you're so young. Otoha Higuchi—is your name by any chance the same as Ichiyo Higuchi, except for the one character?"

"Yes, my mother is a great fan. The story she likes best is *The Thirteenth Night*." She decided to get it all out before being asked.

"My, that's a rather sophisticated choice," Ms. Ninomiya said, slowly leaving the reception area and heading further inside.

"She has a year pass, doesn't she," Otoha said.

"You caught that?"

The pass was hanging on a lanyard around her neck and Otoha had quickly spotted it.

"Her name is Kimiko Ninomiya, and she's a regular," Minami said. "She lives about a fifteen-minute walk from here, and comes nearly every day to spend time where we shelve Konosuke Takagi's work. She never looks at other books."

Konosuke Takagi was a famous novelist of historical fiction. Over twenty years had passed since his death, yet his books continued to sell and be made into movies and dramas.

"Everyone knows this, and I'm sure Ms. Ninomiya talks about it so I don't think she'll mind me mentioning it . . . but she was Mr. Takagi's lover."

"*What . . . ?* His *lover*?"

Her *What?* was more brazen than if she'd screamed.

"Shhh!" Minami, smiling, put a finger up to her mouth.

"I'm sorry, but isn't that insane?"

"It's startling, for sure. When I first heard it, I couldn't believe it myself."

"I've read some of Takagi's works. I really liked his *The Shogun Visits* series."

The Shogun Visits was his best-known work and had been made into a drama twice. As the name suggested it involved a shogun who shows up in neighborhoods in Edo, interacts with ordinary people, and resolves their problems.

"You know what? She said that Takagi bought her a small bar in Ginza back in the day."

"Wow! Sounds like they were lovers for real. Is that all in Wikipedia? Or was it written about in that weekly magazine *Friday*?"

"No, not at all," Minami said. "He was a popular author long ago. Back when there was a taboo about writing gossip about writers. Though she did say it was mentioned once in *The Truth Behind the Rumors*."

"What's that?"

"Maybe you don't know it since you're so young?" Minami said this though she herself was young too. "It's a famous magazine from about twenty years ago. It's not published anymore, but it flouted all the taboos, writing about scandals involving politicians, novelists, and so on. You'll occasionally find copies among the collections of writers here, and that's why I found out about it. I think our library has a complete collection of all the issues. All the people in it are ones from the past, but you can find some interesting stuff."

"Heh!" Otoha exclaimed, again the brazen voice from deep inside her.

"Anyhow, she was Takagi's lover and comes almost every night to visit his collection. She said that being among his books makes her feel like she's with him."

"That's kind of romantic," Otoha said.

"She said that since Takagi had a wife and children, the two of them had to keep things quiet while he was

EPISODE ONE

alive. Still, if you figure his age, they must have started their affair when Mr. Takagi was getting on in years."

"Hmm."

"Anyway, I figure she's sure to tell you about it. It's a long story, but listen to her and pretend you haven't heard it before."

"Roger that!"

As they were talking, another person glided in. A small, thin old lady wearing a light blue smock. She had a woolen hat and a large face mask, as well as fingerless gloves. They couldn't see much of her face, but the white hair of her bowl cut showed her age. Her gait was unexpectedly sure as she crossed the room without a glance at the two of them. After a while she emerged pulling a cart loaded with a large vacuum cleaner and mop. The sound of vacuuming soon came from the room where she was. Most likely she was vacuuming dust from the carpet.

"Who was that?" Otoha asked in a break in their conversation.

"Hmm?"

"The woman who just came in?"

"Oh—Ms. Kobayashi?"

"Her name's Ms. Kobayashi?"

"She's the cleaning lady."

"The cleaning person?"

"She always comes around this time."

"Really? So I should say hello . . ."

Minami shook her head.

"She never talks to people, and if you talk to her she'll rarely answer. So just don't worry about her."

From a kind person like Minami, this sounded a little cold. Maybe she'd been ignored many times and it had hurt her feelings.

"But she's not a bad person and does a wonderful job cleaning." Perhaps noticing Otoha's expression, Minami hurriedly added this. "She also cleans the common areas in our apartment building. You might run across her sometime at the apartment too."

"Really?"

"She's both the library janitor as well as the caretaker of the apartment. So, for instance, if the shared mailboxes are broken she's the one you tell. Though she'll probably not answer you." Minami smiled wryly. "But the next day she'll have it fixed."

"I see."

"So she's a little curt, but don't let it bother you." Minami seemed to be confirming this for herself.

"Ms. Higuchi?" A sudden voice from above made Otoha look up. It was Mr. Sasai.

"I think it's about time you go to the dormitory," he said. "It might be best that you rest up today."

"Oh—thank you very much," Otoha said.

This being her first day working at the office—

working at the library, more accurately—she'd been so excited she hadn't felt sleepy at all and had actually enjoyed herself. But everyone was suggesting she take a break, so she decided to follow their advice.

"Then I'll take you to the dorm."

Mr. Sasai had already been planning to do so from the beginning, since he was wearing a light down coat.

"Thank you so much. But—"

"Yes?"

"I left my coat and bag where Ako and Masako are, so I'll need to fetch them. And I'd like to say goodbye to them."

"I'll wait."

Otoha started to trot off, and Mr. Sasai said from behind, "You don't need to run. Take your time." She instinctively looked back, and he added, "Please don't run in here. Plus ladies don't run. Only children and athletes."

I never saw *that* comment coming, Otoha mused. Conscious of Sasai's and Minami's gaze now, she tiptoed away as quietly as she could.

"Open sesame," she murmured and entered the room where Ako and Masako were.

"I'm sorry, but I'll be leaving for today," she said.

Ako and Masako stood up and looked toward her.

"You came all this way just to say goodbye? You really didn't need to," Ako said cheerfully.

"I had to pick up my bag and coat, too."

"Oh, right."

"Well, see you later!" Masako called out, her hand emerging from the mountain of books to wave.

"Looking forward to being with you tomorrow."

"Have a nice rest."

Otoha bowed several times as she exited the room.

THE APARTMENT WAS ON the grounds of the library. She'd already been told in the second DM from the library about a dorm room being provided for her there.

The property had numerous trees planted in it, like a little park. The old wooden building was out behind the library, so she and Sasai left and went around back. She spotted the apartment right away, a building with a dark blue roof and white walls.

As she walked with Mr. Sasai she looked back, through the trees, at the rectangular gray library building. It felt amazing that such a nondescript building could house such magnificent collections.

"There are eight rooms in the dorm, all of them occupied now," Sasai explained. "Ako and Masako from the sorting room, Mr. Tokai and Ms. Minami Enokida from second-floor reception, Ms. Mai Kitazato from the first-floor front desk, chef Kinoshita, our other recent hire,

Mr. Tokuda . . . and now you, Ms. Higuchi. You'll be on the second floor."

"You don't live there, Mr. Sasai?" she asked from behind as she pulled along her uncooperative suitcase.

"I live somewhere else nearby."

"Is that right?"

"I shouldn't say this myself, but being the manager, I think it's better I live apart from the staff. Also, the dorm is full up," Sasai said.

"I see."

When they went up the stairs Sasai carried the suitcase for her. On the second floor he put a key into the second room on the right.

"Mr. Tokai and chef Kinoshita live downstairs, as generally we put the men on the first floor. But we also thought it best to have Ako and Masako on the first floor, just in case something happens," he said opening the door and then handing Otoha the key.

"By *just in case* you mean—?"

"Earthquakes or fires and such."

"For sure."

Better for older people to be on the first floor.

"This building was built forty-eight years ago. It's old, but the inside's been renovated," Sasai said, clicking on the light. "We've already arranged for the electricity and water to be in your name."

They'd already told her this when they got in touch with her.

"Thank you very much," Otoha said.

"For the gas account, you need to call the company yourself tomorrow."

It was indeed an older building, but the walls were nicely painted white, with upgraded flooring. It was set up as a 1K-type apartment—kitchen plus one room. The bath and the toilet were separate. Old, but more spacious than newer places. In the back was a small closet, or perhaps storage area, about six feet by three feet in size, which must have been a renovated *oshiire*, a closet for storing a futon.

The kitchen was about twelve feet by six feet and rather dated, but it did have a gas range. The eight–tatami mat–sized main room had an AC unit. It was all just as the owner had explained to her earlier. She felt relieved she could start living there right away.

"Your things arrive tomorrow?" Sasai asked.

"Yes. The movers come in the morning. I don't have much, though."

"I've told everyone you'll be moving in, but please try to keep it quiet if you could. They might all still be sleeping. They're not the type to mind it much, though."

"Understood."

"Oh—"

Sasai held a hand to his head.

"There's no futon for tonight."

"I'm okay," Otoha said. "I'll figure something out. The movers are coming at nine tomorrow and after that I'll rest until it's time to go to work."

Sasai still looked troubled. "My apologies. I didn't notice. I'm very sorry."

"Truly, I'm fine."

"No, that's not good. You'll be full of aches and pains, and it's cold, besides."

He opened the closet, searching for something she could use. There was a cardboard box inside.

"Oh, I forgot to tell you about this," Sasai said. "The former resident forgot to take it. Left it behind for some reason . . . I've gotten in touch with her and she should be coming by to pick it up."

"Is that right?"

"Sorry, but could you keep it here until then? Her name is Ms. Saho Oda."

"Of course."

What kind of person would leave behind her belongings like that? Otoha wondered.

But the lack of bedding for Otoha for tonight seemed to bother Sasai more than the left-behind box. *This won't do, won't do at all*, he kept on muttering.

"I'm fine. Really. I'll figure it out for tonight," Otoha said.

Hearing her determined tone, Sasai stopped pacing the room.

"Make sure you don't catch a cold. Be sure to turn on the heat." That's all he said before leaving.

AFTER HE WAS GONE Otoha suddenly felt drained, and slumped down on the kitchen floor, exhaling deeply.

So many things happened today, she thought. *I've come down from my hometown, so far away, been introduced to all those new people, and had the staff dinner . . . and I'm worn out.* Not an unpleasant tiredness, though, at least for now.

She quickly grew sleepy and lay down, still dressed. She removed her coat and used that to cover herself up.

She closed her eyes and soon fell fast asleep.

After a short while she was awakened by a knock at her door. She opened her eyes in the darkness and for a moment wondered where she was. After a minute she remembered: this was the first day in her new workplace.

The knock came again. She glanced at her watch and saw only twenty minutes had passed since Mr. Sasai had left.

". . . Who is it?" she asked in a shaky voice, but got no reply.

She quietly stood up, went to the door and looked through the peephole. No one was there. She shivered, and thought of ignoring it and going back to sleep but summoned her courage and opened the door. At her feet she discovered a sleeping bag.

"Oh . . ."

Maybe Sasai, or another staff member, had left it. She hurried out in her bare feet and looked out the window in the second-floor corridor and saw Sasai quickly walking away from the building.

She wanted to call out to him to thank him but remembered it was late and decided against it. I'll thank him tomorrow—no, *today*, technically—when I see him at the library, she decided, and picked up the sleeping bag.

She looked after his retreating figure again and murmured, "Thank you."

WRAPPED IN THE WARM sleeping bag Otoha had a short dream.

Less a dream, really, than a replay of memories, her thoughts appearing visually to her.

The time she went to inform her parents she'd quit the bookstore.

". . . Are you sure it's okay?" her mother asked, frowning at the thought. "Working in that strange library out in the countryside? And living there too, if you can imagine?"

It's much more the middle of nowhere here, Otoha thought,

though she knew it was possible that the library's location, deep in the Musashino mountains outside of Tokyo, might turn out to be even more rural.

When she didn't reply, her father said in a low voice, "People that don't stick with something for three years aren't worth much."

He stood up and withdrew to an inner room.

Her father was quite strict about things. And she knew his way of thinking was out of date. *Okay*, Otoha wanted to counter, *what if the place you work at turns out to make its employees work overtime for free? Or you encounter sexual harassment there?* But the words didn't come out.

Not that she'd actually faced sexual harassment.

". . . We're just worried about you, Otoha," her Ichiyo Higuchi–loving mother said.

Her mother's bookcase was in the living room and was full of not just Ichiyo Higuchi's works, but all sorts of novels. When Otoha said she wanted to have a job that involved books she'd been even more happy for her daughter, but now this.

"Your work and what you love in life don't have to coincide, you know. For instance, someone who works in the city office yet spends all his free time reading books he enjoys can have a wonderful life. . ." Otoha didn't think her mother's words were wrong, yet she saw that as a way of running away and rejected it. More to the point, she didn't think she'd pass the civil service exam if she decided now to be one.

"I don't want to compromise," Otoha explained.

"So you're saying your father and I compromised in our lives? That we gave up to raise a family?" Her mother's expression changed.

It was hard to imagine it looking at him now, but her father had once played in a band. Her mother, of course, loved literature as a girl. Was she saying she'd given that all up to raise her only daughter and have a family?

"I'm only young once, so let me do what I want to do," Otoha insisted.

". . . Suit yourself," her mother said, fairly spitting out the words.

Otoha felt bad about what she'd said. *I've only ever been trouble and a burden to them*, she thought, *and I don't think I ever once met their expectations. Maybe I'm the one running away.*

The next morning precisely at nine, the mover came. The doorbell rang and Otoha opened it to find a round-faced older man.

"Red Cap Movers!"

"Thank you for coming," Otoha said.

She went with him downstairs, where a red truck was parked.

The man, a veteran mover by the look of it, unloaded

her table, chairs, and plastic cases one after another from the truck, starting with the larger items. Otoha began carrying a cabinet and followed after him.

"You don't need to," he said. "I can handle it all."

He might say that, but she couldn't just stand there doing nothing.

She put the suitcase in her room and went downstairs again and discovered Tokuda, the recently hired older man, and Masako, who had helped her with the stamping, standing next to the truck.

"I'm so sorry—did I wake you?" Otoha hurriedly apologized.

"No, we just thought we might be able to help," Tokuda mumbled.

"I'm fine. He told me he could handle it all."

Despite her words, Tokuda helped bring in the fridge and TV and other large items. He was much kinder than first impressions had led her to believe.

Masako couldn't help move anything, but after Otoha's meager possessions had all been brought inside, she gave the mover a plastic bottle of tea.

"Thank you so much," Masako told him. "You worked so hard. Have this if you'd like."

"Really? Much appreciated." The older man happily accepted the drink.

She's exactly like a kindly grandmother or mother, Otoha thought as she watched her.

EPISODE ONE

"Mr. Tokuda, Masako-san, thank you so much," Otoha said again after the mover had left.

"No problem at all. I wake up at five and can't get back to sleep," Masako said. "And the tea I got for free at a bargain sale at the supermarket. I don't drink that kind of tea myself and it was only taking up space in my fridge."

"I tend to get up early in the morning myself," Tokuda said.

"Would you like to come and have some coffee at my place?" Masako said. "I just brewed some."

"If—you're sure it's okay," Otoha said.

Tokuda, looking a bit unsure, glanced at Otoha. She realized he really wanted to go, but had been hesitating.

"Is it alright if I come too?" Tokuda asked.

MASAKO'S ROOM WAS LAID out exactly like Otoha's, but had a totally different vibe.

There was a low kotatsu table in the middle of the room and a small bookshelf. And over in the kitchen was a large clothes chest and kitchen cabinet. Both were dark brown and sturdy looking and had basically taken over the kitchen. On the floor was a red and green oriental carpet.

It struck Otoha again that it was like going to her grandmother's. And Masako was about the right age for that.

"My parents bought these for me when I was a young woman and I can't bring myself to get rid of them," Masako explained, seeing that Tokuda was looking at the kitchen cabinet.

"Uh—I was just—thinking how we had the same kind of thing in the house I grew up in," Tokuda said.

"Please, sit down in the kotatsu. You must be cold."

As they waited in the kotatsu, Masako brought over coffee in old-fashioned Wedgewood cups. For herself, though, she used a rough mug.

Otoha took a sip and the flavor of the aromatic coffee filled her mouth.

"It's delicious!"

"Really? I'm happy," Masako said. "I bought the beans at a coffee shop near the station. In the mornings I've got to have some tasty coffee. My one little indulgence."

"Thank you for today. Helping me move, and now this delicious coffee," Otoha said.

"And I got some too," Tokuda mumbled, "though I didn't really help out much."

"Not at all. Two women by themselves wouldn't have been able to carry those heavy things. Right?" Masako said looking to Otoha for confirmation.

"That's right. Thank you so much."

"It was nothing." Tokuda was a little bashful.

"Say, why don't you come sometimes in the morning

for coffee?" Masako said to Otoha. "Since I'm up from five. You can have a cup and then go back to sleep until 3:00 p.m., before we have to go to work."

Masako looked back and forth between Otoha and Tokuda.

"You too, of course, Mr. Tokuda."

". . . Okay." Tokuda nodded gravely.

"If it's no trouble for you."

"No, of course not."

"Thank you," Otoha said, nodding.

AFTER ONE CUP OF coffee Otoha returned to her room. She took the futon out of its bag and laid it out beside the sleeping bag Sasai had brought. And without putting out sheets she collapsed onto it.

At long last she felt relieved. She'd finished her first day of work and gotten to know the staff and a couple of the people in the neighborhood.

I think things will work out well, she thought, and sighed a deep, deep sigh.

Nobody here labeled her as gloomy, or cheerful. Nor did they ask why she'd quit the bookstore.

A while ago she'd found the paperback copy of *Shirobanba* next to her sleeping bag. She'd totally forgotten about it. Minami had located a copy and passed it along.

Sprawled on the futon, Otoha opened the book. Scanning the first several pages quickly she soon ran across the description of the rice curry.

> The rice curry the old woman made was delicious. She cut up carrots, daikon, potatoes into cubes, mixed in flour and curry powder, added a bit of canned beef and simmered it all. It had a unique flavor.

Yes, that flavor. That must be the rice curry she'd enjoyed earlier.

Strangely happy, and at peace, she was soon swallowed up by sleep, despite the strong coffee she'd had.

EPISODE TWO

MAMAYA'S CARROT RICE

After moving in, Otoha slept and then went to the library at 3:00 p.m.

When she got there, she spied a large black car parked at the entrance. It was perfectly shiny, and she could tell at a glance it was expensive. She couldn't help peeking inside. An elderly driver was seated there in a suit and black gloves, reading a weekly magazine.

Who had been riding in such a wonderful car? Otoha wondered and was suddenly struck by a thought.

Maybe it was the library's owner?

Despite what Sasai had said, maybe something had brought them here, and if Otoha could meet the owner she might be able to say hello.

She hurried inside.

Sasai was at the reception desk, on the phone, his

expression serious. Beside him stood an elderly man in a navy blue suit. Could *this* be the owner? Otoha thought as she approached them.

He noticed Otoha and nodded to her. When Sasai got off the phone she spoke to him.

"Good morning! Oh—it's not morning, though..."

Otoha realized it was already afternoon, and her hand flew to her mouth in embarrassment.

"How are you doing?" Sasai asked.

"Hmm?"

"How are you doing?"

How are you doing? From this man, in this situation?

"You see, if you say 'how are you doing?' it works whatever the time is."

"I guess you're right..."

"That aside, this is Mr. Kuroiwa, the library's detective," Sasai said. "You haven't met him before, I assume?"

"Correct," Otoha said.

So the man isn't the owner but the library's detective... Goodness, it's one surprise after another here. Otoha stared steadily at him before returning his greeting.

"It's nice to meet you. My name's Kuroiwa."

"Oh. Pardon me. It's nice to meet you. I'm Otoha Higuchi."

"Mr. Kuroiwa is a former policeman. He generally is here during hours when the library is open. You spent most of yesterday in the sorting room so you didn't meet him."

EPISODE TWO

"I see."

"My title is detective," Kuroiwa explained, "but I'm more like a kind of security guard." His voice was low, and calm.

"Today I asked him to come a little early . . . Did you notice the car parked in front of the library?"

"I did!" Otoha exclaimed.

"We have a guest here now."

"Is it the owner?!"

"*Whaat?!*" Mr. Sasai's eyes widened for the first time. He chuckled.

"No, that's not possible . . . That person never comes here. If only that were true . . ."

"So that's not who it is . . ." Otoha's head drooped. "And I wanted to meet the owner so much."

"Unfortunately, there's a sort of difficult patron who's come, so if would excuse me. Mr. Kuroiwa, please come with me."

Sasai and Detective Kuroiwa set off together toward the collections sorting room.

Otoha had brought back the sleeping bag she'd borrowed from Sasai but missed her chance to return it. He must have noticed but had said nothing. Was the patron that important? As she thought this, Otoha placed the sleeping bag at her feet at the reception desk.

As if taking his place, Minami emerged from the staff

room, perhaps now the most familiar face to Otoha. She was carrying a tray with cups of tea.

"Minami-san, good morning. No—I mean . . . Anyway, how are you doing?"

"Oh, Otoha-chan, how are *you* doing?"

"I heard there's a guest?"

Otoha asked because Minami looked even more troubled than Sasai.

"Yes, all of sudden. A short time ago . . ." Minami lowered her voice.

"Who is it? Mr. Sasai said it's a difficult person."

"He said that? Then I guess it's okay to tell you."

Minami motioned her over and when she got closer whispered in her ear, "It's the writer Junichiro Tamura."

"Junichiro Tamura?"

Everyone in this field knew the name, for he was a famous writer. He would be about seventy now, and had been publishing one hit novel after another since he was young. Even now if he published a new work, it was sure to be on the bestseller list for a few weeks.

Plus . . . Even someone like Otoha, a bookstore employee from an off-the-beaten-track kind of place, knew this writer to be notoriously, resoundingly cranky and difficult.

On TV and other media he came across as a vibrant, broad-minded older man, but with editors it was said he did a one-eighty, becoming difficult, overbearing, selfish—a person who spoke his mind and damn the consequences.

". . . But why would he be here at our place?" Otoha asked.

She suddenly realized that, though it was only her second day, she was referring to the workplace as *our place*. She felt a bit embarrassed, but Minami didn't seem to notice.

"I have no idea. They said he's been here before we came to work. Ms. Kitazato from reception and Mr. Sasai have been taking care of him in the drawing room. And Mr. Sasai's making a call somewhere. Anyway, I'll take the tea over. They asked me to."

"I'm going to go change," Otoha said.

"Good. Could you help out at the reception desk?"

"Sure. But now that you mention it, where is the drawing room?"

"On the second floor next to the cafe. When the cafe's open Mr. Kinoshita can provide coffee too."

"Ah, so that's where it is . . ."

She saw Minami off to the second floor and then hurried toward the collections sorting room. Yesterday Masako and Ako had told her to use the lockers there when she was sorting out collections.

This is serious. Serious indeed. Before she'd realized it, she'd been muttering this to herself. She opened the bookshelf and went inside, where she found Masako and Ako, Sasai and Detective Kuroiwa, all huddled together.

"That's kind of sudden to be told that . . ." she heard Masako say as she tilted her head in doubt.

"We haven't yet sorted out the cardboard boxes. It's only been a few weeks since he passed away. We received them actually pretty quickly."

"So what did he say?" Ako said. Her back was to the entrance and Sasai shook his head a little, as if to indicate Otoha's presence to her. Ako turned around.

"Oh. Otoha. Good morning."

"I'm sorry to interrupt."

Clearly something out of the ordinary was going on here, and Otoha stiffened.

"It's okay," Masako said, quickly pulling herself together.

"I'm going to put my things down . . . and put on my apron . . . I was asked to sit at the reception desk," Otoha said.

With all four staring at her, she felt flustered.

"It's okay, Mr. Sasai. Otoha should hear this too. She's on the staff now, and it has to do with collection sorting."

"You're right. Why don't we tell you about it as you change."

"Alright."

Otoha left her bag and coat in the locker in the corner and took out her apron.

"That car parked out front is actually Junichiro Tamura's."

"I heard a little bit about that from Minami," Otoha said, nodding. She was having a hard time tying her apron strings behind her back, so Ako came around behind her and helped her. When she finished, she gave Otoha a gentle pat on the back, as if to say *Everything's alright*.

"Mr. Tamura barged right in without any warning, saying he wanted us to show him some books."

"Some . . . books?" Otoha said.

Well this was a library, after all, so asking to see books seemed quite natural.

"The thing is, he wants us to show him Tadasuke Shirakawa's books."

"Tadasuke Shirakawa? . . . And that would be . . .?"

"Yes, people your age, Otoha, might not know him."

The past lives on here in this library, she thought. And how many times had she heard that since yesterday? *People your age, Otoha, might not know*.

I wish I could be older, she suddenly thought. Get older . . . gain more experience and she could be a full-fledged part of their group.

Her parents had long told her, "If you don't decide

soon, you'll get older and won't be able to have a decent job." Though she knew that all too well.

Not just when it came to jobs, but now that she'd reached her mid-twenties she was well aware, as a woman, that thirty was just around the corner.

And here she was thinking, if only for a moment, that she'd like to be *older*.

"Both Mr. Tamura and Mr. Shirakawa were recipients of the Kanto Literary Prize. And at the same time."

"Ah, the Kanto . . ."

The Kanto Prize was a prize for new writers sponsored by a medium-size publisher. It was still being awarded.

"But isn't the Kanto Prize for literary fiction?" Otoha asked.

"That's right," Sasai broke in. "At the time Mr. Tamura, too, was a writer of literary fiction."

"Huh. I had no idea."

"Mr. Shirakawa's piece was also nominated for the Akutagawa Prize. Though he unfortunately didn't win, it was widely praised and his career was set after that."

"I see."

"Mr. Tamura, on the other hand, went through some hard times. No matter how much he wrote he couldn't even get his work published in the magazine that had published his first, prize-winning story. It was one rejection slip after another."

Ako gave a small shrug, and murmured, "Maybe that's what made his personality all twisted."

"Shhh," Masako said, putting a finger to her lips.

"No, I heard that he was quite pleasant back then. And very serious. At any rate, he tried his best." This from Sasai.

"But then an editor suggested he write more commercial-type novels and his career blossomed. The very first novel of that type he wrote caught the eye of a famous critic, who praised it to the skies and it became a moderate hit. You know what happened after that. And it was around that time that his personality got so warped . . ."

"Even *you* think that, Mr. Sasai?" Masako said, frowning.

"I think when people suffer for a long time and then are suddenly made much of, it can twist them."

"That makes sense."

"This is a well-known story, but Mr. Tamura liked mountain climbing and he forced his editors to come along. He told them he'd write his next work for whoever made it to the top first, forcing them to compete with each other. One of the editors took a tumble and was badly injured. Or else, the other version of the story was that Mr. Tamura's hat blew off, and he said he'd publish with whoever retrieved it and one of the editors fell from a cliff and broke his leg. . . At any rate, it's hard to say what really happened, but tons of rumors like that swirled about him."

"Well, rumors are rumors, and our task right now is to think about what to do," Masako said decisively.

"Why does he want to view Mr. Shirakawa's books? Were the two of them close?" Otoha hesitantly asked.

"There's a backstory to that, actually," Ako said, frowning. "After Mr. Tamura was successful with his entertainment novels, Mr. Shirakawa wrote an essay for a newspaper. Talk about scathing. The title was *Thou Shalt Not Die*, obviously taken from Akiko Yosano's famous poem about her brother going off to war. Kind of overblown, wouldn't you say?

"Mr. Shirakawa wrote that his rival was now mass-producing awful work, and how disappointed that made him. He believed it was the same as Mr. Tamura being dead . . . 'at least don't die any more than you already have,' he said. He also said that Tamura did it hoping to someday surpass him, but he never would at that rate. Remarks of that nature."

"Thus the title *Thou Shalt Not Die*?" Otoha said.

"After that, their relationship seemed to turn hostile. Or maybe not, really, since they never had any contact. The world they each occupied was so different. Mr. Tamura was the popular author while Mr. Shirakawa . . . unfortunately never did win the Akutagawa Prize for serious fiction, and while he's continued to publish short stories in literary magazines over the past ten years, he hasn't put out a single book. Since it wouldn't sell well. His reputation, though, remains high."

"I love his writing," Ako continued. "It's so serene and proud, yet strikingly new, always full of surprises . . . Every time I read his work I'm impressed at how he discovers the truths still hidden away in people and their lives. Whenever a literary journal has a story of his in it, I always buy it and read it."

Just then the door opened and Minami came in.

"We need you, Mr. Sasai, or someone else, to come," she said. "Mr. Tamura's upset at being made to wait so long and I can't handle it."

"Oh, sorry about that. I'll go," Sasai said.

Minami and Sasai left, with Kuroiwa tagging along. If Tamura was about to kick up a fuss that's where his skill set kicked in.

". . . I guess I'll be off to the reception desk to help Minami," Otoha said.

"Good idea. Thanks, Otoha."

"But where are Mr. Shirakawa's books right now?"

Masako shook her head.

"They haven't come here yet and are still stacked up in the warehouse. It's a huge number of books. There are other people's collections there, too, and probably the earliest we could get them all organized would be in a few months."

"I see. Well, I'll be off," Otoha said and exited the room.

AT THE RECEPTION DESK she found Minami, the tray tucked under her arm, and Tokai, who'd just come to work, huddled together as they were when she first met them. They were whispering. Something about Mr. Tamura would be her guess.

Noticing Otoha, Minami nodded once.

"Is everything okay?" Otoha asked.

"Um. When I made tea for him, he asked, 'How long are you going to make me wait?' But the way he said it, in this low voice, was so scary."

Otoha remembered that Mr. Tamura's forte was heroic stories and detective stories.

Tokai shook his head. "If Mr. Tamura said that to me, I'd shake all over," he said.

"How did he seem when he first came here?"

". . . The first one here was Mai Kitazato, who works at the entrance. She always arrives thirty minutes before work starts at four and unlocks the front door. According to her, that black car was already parked outside then."

"Really?"

"Mr. Tamura got really upset then. 'What are you people doing?' he said. 'How long are you going to keep me waiting here?'"

EPISODE TWO

"Had he gotten in touch beforehand?"

"No. But he said if you're going to call this place a library you should be open during the day. He'd come over without checking our library hours and I think he felt a bit embarrassed."

"I see."

He did have a point. Tamura was all worked up, ready to charge inside, only to find the library closed.

"Ms. Kitazato kept him from barging right in and they got into a bit of squabble right there in front of the library entrance. That's when Mr. Sasai showed up."

"Really? Ms. Kitazato really confronted him like that all by herself?"

"She's a ranked karate athlete, remember."

"Oh, that's right."

"Nothing gets to her."

"Does that have something to do with karate?" Otoha asked.

"Not really. Normally she doesn't talk a lot, though sometimes it's fun to talk with her. One sort of pet phrase of hers is 'I know where people are most vulnerable.'"

"Whoa!"

"Anyway, Mr. Sasai decided he'd better let him in and took him to the drawing room, and that's when we came."

"Mr. Shirakawa's books would be where now . . . ?" Tokai, silent until now, asked this.

"They're still in the warehouse. And there are lots of them," Otoha said, repeating what she'd just heard.

"Is that so? So what're we going to do?"

As they were talking, Mr. Sasai came down from the second floor, a stern look on his face. He probably wasn't aware of it himself, but he let out a small sigh. He was suddenly surprised to notice the three of them looking at him and came over to the reception desk.

"How did it go?" Minami said, taking the plunge.

"I told him that we haven't organized Mr. Shirakawa's books yet, that it will take a few months to do that, but that he would be the first to know when they're ready. But he wouldn't budge, insisting he has to see Mr. Shirakawa's books today."

"My goodness, that's so selfish," Minami said, not mincing her words.

"He's quite a busy person, of course, and can't be expected to come often to this out-of-the-way place." For all the problems he'd caused, Sasai was still defending him, to some extent.

"I told him it'll take several hours for us to take them out of the warehouse and arrange the books here and that since there are so many volumes he'd need plenty of time to go through them."

"Where is the warehouse located?"

To Otoha's question, Sasai exchanged a look with Tokai and Minami, and let out another sigh.

EPISODE TWO

". . . It's quite a ways from here. We're using an old house in the mountains in Oume as our warehouse. It takes about an hour by car, so if we drive there, load the books and then drive back . . ."

"It'll take two and a half hours, at least."

"Mr. Tamura said that's fine with him and told us to go."

"I see."

"Masako and Ako are in charge of sorting collections, but they can't handle all that, just the two of them. It's far away and there'll be a lot of hard work with so many books. So I'll go, with Mr. Tokai, Mr. Tokuda . . . and . . ."

Sasai's eyes came to rest on Otoha.

Huh? *Me?* Otoha said, pointing to herself.

"Could you accompany us too, Ms. Higuchi? You've never been to the warehouse, and it's a good opportunity for you."

"Wouldn't it be better to have Detective Kuroiwa go with you?" Tokai said, sympathizing with Otoha.

"No, I'd like Mr. Kuroiwa to stay here, just in case. If Mr. Tamura starts to act up again there could be trouble. He's the type who lords it over women . . ."

"I see."

Otoha knew only too well how an arrogant person with a complaint would dig in their heels even more if they were dealing with a woman. She'd seen this countless times at the bookstore.

"I have him stationed outside the drawing room, just in case."

"Alright," Otoha said. "I'll go with you. I'd like to see the warehouse."

"It's terribly cold today and the warehouse is in an even colder place. It doesn't have much in the way of heating so let's make sure to bundle up. If you need to bring something warmer you should go back to the dorm and fetch it."

"I wore my down jacket, so I'll be fine," Otoha said.

"Then let's head out. Can we bring it all back in one car?"

Sasai inclined his head doubtfully.

"The library has a HiAce van, and I'll bring my car around too. It's just a regular sedan, though," Tokai said.

"Then we should be able to manage. We'll bring the cars around front so please go get Mr. Tokuda."

Sasai turned to Minami.

"Make sure you bring him tea regularly. Mr. Kinoshita will come to work soon, and then you can ask Mr. Tamura if he'd like some coffee and if he does bring some to him from the cafe."

"Roger!" Minami gave a funny little salute.

"If you have any problems, ask Masako and Ako. And you can call my cell."

"Aye-aye, sir!"

One more salute from Minami.

As she waited with Tokuda at the entrance, two cars rolled up. Tokuda got into the passenger side of Tokai's car as if that were expected, so Otoha got in the passenger seat of the HiAce.

"Shall I turn on the radio?" Sasai asked after Otoha had removed her coat and put it on the rear seat.

"Yes, please."

The thought of being with Sasai for the one-hour drive there—two hours if you counted both ways—left her a bit tense.

"What kind of music do you usually listen to?" Sasai asked her.

"Any kind is fine," Otoha said.

"Then I'll choose something."

Sasai chose the NHK station, and the sudden sound of a classical string quartet surprised her, though he seemed unfazed.

". . . Does this sort of thing happen often? That writers show up like this?" Otoha asked after a while, when the silence between them was getting to her.

"No, it doesn't. At most maybe two or three times a year . . . Most writers just show up without telling us, examine books like any other library patron, and then leave, so we never even notice their presence."

"I would imagine so."

"We've had a few times when they've gotten in touch beforehand. They come to gather material for their own writing, and some would-be writers come to check out other writers' collections, thinking it might be helpful. Some come simply as fans. And some come to check out how their books will be dealt with after their death. But that happens very rarely."

"I suppose so."

Silence again descended.

". . . Um, this might sound strange, but do you mind if I ask a question?" Otoha asked hesitantly.

"Ask whatever you like. I hope I can answer it."

"How does this library . . . get by? It's not that I'm concerned about it, it's my parents. They were a little worried about how a private library manages to operate."

"Ah, right." Sasai nodded. "The operations are a bit odd, admittedly. No wonder your parents are worried."

"It doesn't bother me—seriously. If, by any chance, anything happened I think I can always go back home and find work."

Oops, now I've said it, Otoha thought, a bit flustered. "I'm not implying I'm working here sort of half-heartedly or came here feeling that way. Just working here yesterday I've found it a lovely place and if possible, I'd love to work here for a long time. Which is exactly why I'm a bit concerned about how you manage." As she spoke she found herself growing breathless.

"I understand. Of course I do."

Since Sasai was facing forward it was hard to tell, but he seemed to be smiling wryly.

"You seem to worry too much about things, Ms. Higuchi. You're quite the empathetic type, I take it. Just relax and say whatever you want to say to us."

"The empathetic type . . .? Thank you for pointing that out."

No one had ever said that to her at work before.

"I might be a little insensitive myself. I wouldn't call Masako and Ako insensitive, but as you get older you find yourself ready for anything. My advice? Just do your work and don't worry so much."

"*You? Insensitive?!* I don't think so at all." She couldn't help laughing. "But I just came here yesterday so there's so much I still don't know."

"My relatives, though, have told me I'm thickheaded," Sasai said.

"No way!"

"Well—whatever. Anyway, don't worry too much about things. We'll be working together for quite some time, so let's just take it easy at work."

"I really appreciate your saying that." Before Otoha knew it she was bowing deeply to him from the passenger seat.

"To get back to what we were saying . . .?"

"Uh . . . right. According to what I heard, the building itself was apparently built into a library as a kind of hobby by a person who'd made a fortune in real estate in the past, in the so-called Bubble Era. But when the bubble economy burst he went bankrupt, the building was put up for sale, but the owners couldn't find a good use for it and it changed hands a number of times. I heard it was basically in ruins and abandoned at the end when it was bought again cheaply and renovated. The same for the apartment building out back. At first the library took in a few authors' collections, with the owner getting them organized, and then a few years ago Ryoichi Kaito came along."

This was an author whose works had been widely translated into English and sold well abroad, and he had sold even more after he'd been nominated for the Nobel Prize. The author had passed away five years ago.

"It was after his death, after he'd willed his collection to us, that we finally started getting a steady stream of patrons coming here. Since Kaito was famous abroad, and owned plenty of English books, we also had quite a number of guests from abroad. Something we were quite grateful for. Though his collection was later stolen and put up for auction, which made a bit of a splash in the news."

"Is that what happened?"

"Ever since then, we beefed up security at the entrance, and hired Kuroiwa as our detective. But you know, that incident was a lucky break in a way, as it got our name out there. To an extent, running the library got easier. The number of authors and their families who donated their collections also increased. Among them were some who willed us a part of their estate to help us continue operations . . . And we also received support from the government for the preservation of cultural properties."

"Really?"

"Even so, it's true that most of our operating funds have come from the owner's personal assets."

"Eh? Is that right?" The owner's own funds?

"Actually . . . yes."

"Hmm."

"Mr. Tamura told me that if we were able to show him Mr. Shirakawa's collection today he'd donate his own collection, as well as give a substantial monetary donation."

"Wow."

"Well, you know, I'm not about to go to all this trouble for nothing." Sasai gave a rare laugh. "Apparently his collection contains the multivolume *Unabridged Japanese Language Dictionary*—a complete set, in mint condition."

"That's the most expensive dictionary in Japan, isn't

it. I must say, Mr. Sasai, I didn't expect you to be such a go-getter." *Oh no!* she thought, hand flying back to her mouth. *Again blurting out something I shouldn't have!* "I'm sorry, I went a bit overboard there."

"It's okay. I take it as a compliment. Don't let it bother you. I'm happy to hear that."

"Well, thank you for saying that."

Quiet classical music filled the car for a while.

"Why not take a nap if you'd like, Ms. Higuchi. You must be worn out after yesterday. With moving in and all."

"No, I'm fine. I slept quite well after I finished moving."

"But there's still some time before we get there, and once we do, I'll keep you busy."

She was determined not to fall asleep, but Mr. Sasai gentle tone lulled her and before she knew it, she had slipped into a deep slumber.

I'M NOT THAT GOOD *of a person or have my act together. Most of all, I'm not a happy person.*

These thoughts ran through my mind as I sent off Sasai, Otoha, and Tokai as they quickly drove away.

Aye-aye, sir! Now where had *that* come from? I'd burst out with that before I knew it.

Somehow, after seeing all four of them off as *cheerfully* as I could, I felt exhausted . . .

EPISODE TWO 81

My, my . . . I sighed, and unsteadily sat down at the reception desk.

"Ms. Minami Enokida."

Taken by surprise by the voice behind me, I spun around.

Masako and Ako were standing there.

"Are you okay by yourself?"

"I'm good!" I said. I smiled broadly and gave a thumbs-up.

"You sure? . . . You seem a bit down . . . Tell us if you're tired, okay? And about Mr. Tamura." Masako pointed upstairs. "If he says anything, just tell us."

"Can you really handle it by yourself?" Ako asked, clearly worried.

"Well . . ."

Truth be told, I didn't want to be left alone, and wished someone could be by my side. That man . . . No, that *old* man . . . Junichiro Tamura, was pretty scary. If he yells at me one more time, I might burst into tears. *If he says anything, just tell us.* All well and good, but I need someone next to me at *that moment*, since I don't think I can handle him all by myself . . . I'm scared I can't do it on my own, and even Tokai's away now, gone off to the warehouse.

"I'm good!" I said again, smiling, the words at odds with my feelings. This time I gave two thumbs-up, which transitioned into a couple of fist pumps.

"That old man—I'll clean his clock."

"You don't need to go *that* far."

Masako burst out laughing. "Uh, alright. But I'm not about to lose out to him."

"It's okay to lose," Ako said.

Her words took me by surprise. "Huh?"

"Well, we'll be in the sorting room."

The two of them left, apparently not noticing the expression on my face.

What did Ako mean by *It's okay to lose*? This question swirling in my head, I got the reception desk ready to go. Come storm, come snow, come oddball novelist, the library must be ready for business.

I fired up the computer and straightened up the desk. I needed to reply to the inquiries that came in via the library's public email address. Usually, these questions concerned collections and authors they dealt with.

> I'm looking into the author Kiyotaka Ishikawa from Saitama Prefecture. Does his collection contain any books related to the medical field? If it does, could you please create a list of these and send it to me?

Most likely a person from the same area looking into local history, I figured. In most cases these types of inquiries were from retired high school history teachers and the like who, after retirement, styled themselves as researchers.

No idea, you pest, I inwardly cursed.

This isn't a public library, and I am no volunteer. So why did I have to create and send a list just because this researcher poser I didn't know from Adam sent in a request?

Handling such reference requests was one of the main tasks of a librarian, of course, but did I really have to go to all that trouble here?

> If among the list there are some interesting-looking books, I am willing to go visit directly to look into them further.

What? Is he saying that if they have some useful material he doesn't mind *deigning* to come check them out? This guy's definitely a teacher . . . or a scholar. With that superior attitude he's gotta be.

But I couldn't very well ignore him. I searched for the list of books in this Kiyotaka Ishikawa's collection and forwarded it to him, making my reply as superficially polite as I could.

> Thank you very much for your recent inquiry. I began the task of selecting medical-related books from the

> list of Kiyotaka Ishikawa's collection, but I realized that, not being well-versed in that field, I might well overlook some items, and I felt it best to send you the entire catalogue of his holdings...

Naturally all the books had index and classification numbers, so it would be possible to use the search function to create a list. But this sender's brazenness offended me, the way he expected an instant response to his requests.

Irritated, I typed and sent my reply. I'd expected to feel refreshed getting that off my plate, but with the faint *whoosh* as the reply was sent, I felt even more irritated than before.

At times like these, I wondered whether I really did like books and book-related work.

I was a very meek child growing up. I hated parks and playgrounds. I was clumsy, far from athletic, would inevitably fall if I ran, jam a finger if I tried to catch a ball, and would fall off jungle gyms, overhead ladders, and horizontal bars. If I didn't want to get hurt, the only alternative was to stay home and read books. For better or worse, my parents, too, loved books.

With such praise from them ringing in my head—*You really love books, don't you, Minami, You're so good in Japanese class, You should really become a teacher or a librarian*—I chose to major in English in college, and got certified as both a librarian and a teacher. I was certified to be a teacher but didn't want to be one. I'd never enjoyed academic life, and the thought of returning to it made me shudder.

Though I'd graduated from a mid-level university in Tokyo, I couldn't find work as a librarian and ended up working part-time at a suburban public library. Part-time employment, though, was always capped at three months. There were libraries scattered throughout the city, and I moved from one to the other every three months. There were several other people following the same track. City libraries managed to get by that way, though no one ever tried to improve the system.

When I was interviewed, I was asked if I was okay with working as a part-timer, not a full-fledged librarian. In other words, not hired as a specialist but to do a job anybody could handle. There were no other job prospects, so I had no choice.

Truth be told, though, I wasn't so set on getting full-time work. Here minimum wage was guaranteed, but they couldn't pay a high salary. The days and hours I worked each month were fixed, and anything beyond that was unpaid overtime. After retirement and medical were deducted I was left with about ¥120,000 deposited monthly into my account. I lived at home with my parents, and with my mom making a lunch for me to take each day I could manage to get by. I gave my parents ¥30,000 each month for expenses but could still buy a few extras I liked and put away a bit in savings. And I didn't mind when my parents told people that their daughter worked in a city public library. As I lived this life, I figured I'd eventually meet someone and get married.

I went on social media, introducing myself as a librarian in a countryside library, part-time. My username was *South*. Actually I lived in suburbs of the Kanto area, but out of caution I pretended online to be living in some outlying region of the country. I didn't post much, the occasional photos of cakes, and cafes, my thoughts on novels I'd read. In a few years I'd gathered a few hundred followers. Just your average, low-key social media presence.

One day, without much aforethought, I posted about my situation. How city rules capped part-time work of any kind at three months max and how I had, for several years, worked in this system where, when your time was up, you had just a few days off and then moved on to another library. And how you couldn't ever expect the compensation to rise above the set take-home pay of ¥120,000 per month . . . I'd written it all self-deprecatingly, but the post was suddenly picked up.

A male influencer online retweeted my post, adding comments that something was fundamentally wrong, structurally, with Japan if it treated a woman like this, a college graduate qualified to be both a teacher and librarian. This post got even more readers.

Honestly, I hadn't written it to complain about anything and was confused by the reaction. If it spread any more and got to be a social issue, I was thinking of deleting my account, but things died down after a couple days, with around two thousand likes and a few hundred retweets. The whole thing basically blew over.

Just as I was feeling relieved it was finished, I received a message inviting me to work at the night library.

> Hello. I've been reading all your tweets. My username is Seven Rainbows. I was surprised recently when I read your tweet, South, about your work in a library. If you'd like, I can introduce you to a job related to books. Would that be alright?

What attracted me to the job wasn't the duties of working in a library, or the unique nature of the place with its holdings of authors' personal collections, but rather the conditions. The salary was ¥30,000 more per month than I'd been getting, and they offered a free dorm room. These days my parents had been putting more pressure on me to *Get married!* It was depressing, and if I was bound to get married anyway I wanted to try, for a time, living on my own first.

So the reasons I came here were, admittedly, rather passive ones.

But I found this library easier to work in than I'd

imagined. Work was laid-back, and the rest of the staff were kind to me.

Until Otoha came, I was the youngest staff member. I grew used to acting like the "youngest child" at work. The lineup here were the much older Masako and Ako, quiet Mr. Sasai, Tokai, more like an older brother (Tokuda still hadn't started when I was hired), and I felt what was missing was a forever-cheerful, impish kid sister. Before I knew it, I'd started acting that way.

But now, replying to this selfish patron's email, I felt my true nature rising to the fore and it frightened me.

I'm completely different from the others working in this library . . .

Tokuda, who'd started after me, and Otoha, who'd only started yesterday, made no effort to hide the fact they *Love books!* and *Love novels more than anything!*

I, on the other hand, only read what's necessary to do my job, and don't study beyond that, though the amount of reading required is great enough to give others the impression I'm quite the reader.

But someday, won't my false front be ripped away revealing who I really am?

I live in constant dread of this.

"Ms. Higuchi, we'll be arriving in a minute."

Sasai's voice woke her up and Otoha saw they were

on a road in the mountains, everything around pitch-black. Instinctively she looked behind them, where Tokai's car was keeping pace. Except for that everything was covered in darkness.

"Sorry. I fell asleep."

"It's okay. I told you you should."

"This is quite a place."

"Believe it or not, it's still part of Tokyo."

A hamlet appeared as they emerged from the woods and Sasai stopped the car in front of one of the wooden houses. It was a two-story farmhouse surrounded by a bamboo forest. It had a large garden, part of which was a cultivated field.

"Wait here for a minute, please," he said.

Sasai got down from the driver's seat, walked to the rear of the van and took out two flashlights. One he handed to Tokai, the other he switched on, then opened the passenger door and shone it on the ground below.

"Thank you," Otoha said.

She ducked her head as the cold air rushed in. The night library was well on the outskirts of the city, and plenty cold, but here, she felt, was even more chilly.

"It's pitch-black, so watch your step," Sasai cautioned.

The four of them followed the light from the flashlights to the door of the farmhouse-like building, where Sasai inserted a key and with a clatter slid open the door.

This is still, technically, a part of Tokyo, but it's a lot like my hometown, Otoha mused. Though her home was a condo in the local town, a lot of her friends had homes like this.

"So the warehouse is here?" she asked.

"It is. This is one of the houses the owner liked and bought. There's also a storehouse out back, so you should be able to keep books there too," he said.

"I see."

"It looks just like an average wooden building, and since it's old you'd think there might be a problem with moisture and so on, but it's quite solid for a wood frame house. Even so, the owner said the plan is to eventually purchase a real warehouse and move the holdings there."

"I see, but boy is it cold here," Tokai said, to which Tokuda nodded.

"I'll turn on the lights."

Sasai switched on the front door lights with a *click* and everything brightened. Otoha let out a sigh. The light alone made it seem a tad warmer.

The entrance was a spacious packed dirt floor, as big as Otoha's room in the dorm. A carved wooden statue of a hawk, perhaps the former owner's, adorned the room.

Sasai slid open another door and there was an extensive room with a sunken hearth in the center.

Tokuda, quiet until now, spoke up. "This is wonderful. I could see it becoming a Japanese inn."

EPISODE TWO

"Is this your first time here, too, Mr. Tokuda?" Otoha asked.

"No, I came here once before, but we went straight back to the annex to pick up a collection."

"There's an annex?"

"Yes, a sort of guest cottage out back."

There was a kitchen next to the room with the sunken hearth, and behind that two Japanese-style rooms full of cardboard boxes.

"This is Mr. Shirakawa's collection."

"Wow, so that's it."

"Anyway, let's start moving them."

"Like this? Isn't it too cold?" Tokuda said, pouting.

"Okay, we'll turn on the heater first. We put in this heater when we renovated the house, just in case. It's small and doesn't work that well. It might not heat up the place while we're moving out the boxes."

Even so, Sasai went to locate the switch and turned it on. The heater, set in a corner of the room, came on with a strange buzzing sound, and indeed all it did was send out air. It actually made the room seem even colder.

"Masako and Ako told me there are twenty-three boxes total in Mr. Shirakawa's collection. His name is written on the top and side of each box."

"This is one, right?"

Otoha located one of them.

"All of these here must be his," Sasai said.

"There's so many," Otoha exclaimed.

"It's about average for an author."

Silently, they set about carrying out the boxes. They gave Otoha the smaller ones, telling her not to overdo it, but even they were heavy, packed full of books.

The room never seemed to warm up, the cold rising from their feet and leaving them chilled to the bone. Walking on the wooden floor felt like ice-skating barefoot. Otoha regretted just wearing one pair of socks instead of two.

With all that, going back and forth between the house and the cars, they were able to move out all the boxes in about a half hour. By the end, the room finally seemed to have gotten a little warmer, though it could have been because they'd been moving around so much, Otoha thought. That's how piercingly cold the house was.

THEY WERE MORE SILENT driving back than on the way out. Otoha offered to spot him at the wheel, but Sasai insisted on driving himself.

"It's the outskirts, but it's still Tokyo," he said, "and it's unfair to make someone drive who only just arrived yesterday. And I don't mind driving all that much."

Otoha had driven back home, even taking up the

challenge of mountain roads at times and was confident in her driving skills, but she didn't insist.

They stopped once at a convenience store, taking turns using the restroom, and had a hot cup of coffee.

"Maybe we could find a family restaurant somewhere and have a bite to eat?" Tokai suggested, but Sasai shook his head and took out his cell phone.

There'd been several calls from Masako, as well as a short text from Minami.

"I called Masako back a while ago and she said that Mr. Tamura had about reached the end of his rope."

"I see."

Minami's short text said, How many more minutes before you get back? He told me he dislikes coffee. This followed by a series of crying face emojis.

The four of them exchanged a look and let out a collective sigh.

"Let's hurry back as fast as we can, making sure of course not to have an accident or get caught speeding," Sasai said and they all nodded assent.

It was even more silent once they got back in the car. When Otoha spotted the road sign with the name of the town where the library was, she felt relieved.

"There's one thing I wanted to say," Sasai said as the library came into view.

"Yes?"

"That house . . . the one we went to that's used as a warehouse, it actually is a really wonderful building. Today was unfortunately so cold, and you might only have painful memories of it, but I hope you have a chance to go back there sometime when the weather's nicer."

"Is that right? . . . I understand."

Right now, though, she thought, *I certainly don't feel like it.*

THREE PEOPLE WERE WAITING for them at the entrance with pushcart dollies—Masako, Ako, and Minami.

"Thank you so much," Masako said. "Believe me, we were counting the minutes."

"I wanted him to stay in the drawing room," Minami added, "but he started walking around the library, calling writers' names as he spotted their books, things like *That jerk, reading such trash* and *That guy's books didn't sell, yet he read all these difficult books like he's some full-fledged writer or something*. He raked Mr. Kinoshita over the coals, too, about his cafe menu, and they almost came to blows over it." Minami looked disgusted as she related this.

"I'm sorry you had such a hard time. I thought many times I should have turned him down."

"Mr. Kuroiwa stuck close behind him so that made it a little better," Minami said.

"I'm truly sorry." Sasai bowed deeply to her.

"It's not your fault. Well, let's move these inside." Ako alone seemed upbeat.

To get things going, the men unloaded the boxes from the cars onto the dollies.

"Ms. Higuchi, you can go take a break," they all told her, but when she saw that the two boxes on Ako's dolly were unstable and wobbling, she went to lend a hand.

"I'll push it, and could you hold the boxes down, Ako?"

"This box is a bit overstuffed and bulging out, which is why it's wobbling."

They took the elevator to the second floor. When they entered the drawing room they found a thoroughly exhausted Tamura sprawled back on the sofa.

"You finally got here . . ."

Not a word of thanks, which upset Otoha, but then she realized this elderly man had been here since the early afternoon and couldn't help being worn out himself.

Ako and the others silently took the boxes off the carts, stripped the tape off them one by one, and opened them.

"Hold on there . . . you need some, uh, scissors, or maybe a knife . . ." Tamura explained in frustration as Minami struggled with the tight packing tape.

"A box cutter?" Minami asked, her face a blank.

"Right. With a box cutter you could open them up right away."

"But that might damage the books. They're precious, these books! We can't do that," Masako said firmly.

That was enough to silence even Tamura.

Despite his impatience, Tamura didn't touch the boxes, standing by them until they'd all been brought in.

"This is all of them . . ." Sasai said as he opened the last one.

Relief swept over them all. *Boy oh boy, glad that's finally over!* was the unspoken, shared thought.

"Okay. All of you get out now," Tamura commanded. "I'll do the rest myself."

Still no word of thanks, in fact making it sound like they owed *him* one.

"I'm sorry, but we cannot allow that," Masako said firmly again. "We haven't organized Mr. Shirakawa's books yet. Haven't counted how many there are and haven't made an index or list of titles. If any book is lost now there's no way we would know."

"Are you . . . implying *I* might steal a book?"

"I'm just saying some might get lost. Something might happen and a book or two might get misplaced and then we can't locate them. That'll never do."

"Are you accusing me? You think I'm the kind of man who'd steal this idiotic novelist's idiotic books?"

"Man or woman doesn't matter. I'm saying we can't have any books getting lost. Please let someone, even one person, stay behind here with you."

"You want to keep an eye on me because I might steal some of the books from you?"

With each word his voice got stronger, louder, deeper, till at the end he sounded like someone from a yakuza crime movie.

But the reedy Masako was unfazed, even with this big man's sharp voice attempting to browbeat her.

"I never said anything about stealing," she went on. "And the books here are not ours. They're cultural assets that authors have left for us. They're treasures for the Japanese people—no, for *all* humanity. Naturally the same would hold true if you, Mr. Tamura, likewise left us your books, and we would treat them exactly the same. Because we love authors and hold them in the highest regard."

Tamura's face, puffed up with rage and looking ready to burst, suddenly deflated.

"Then . . . you. You can stay." He pointed at Masako. "But no one else."

"Alright."

Sasai stepped forward, about to say something, but Masako stopped him with a shake of her head. "I'll take care of our guest," she said, "so everyone else, please step out."

One by one they filed out, leaving Masako behind in the drawing room.

"Masako is really something else, isn't she," Otoha said.

"Librarians like her from a pre-computer age have a different attitude," Tokai agreed, shaking his head.

"There's a connection?"

"There is. Without computers, Masako and those from that generation had to know the titles, contents, and location of at least five thousand volumes."

"No way!"

When they got back to the reception desk, Detective Kuroiwa was just coming in from outside. He pointed outside with his thumb. "I just heard from the driver . . . that famous author's driver."

Otoha realized that after Kuroiwa had helped unload the cardboard boxes, he must've gone off somewhere.

"Did you find out something?"

"Mr. Kinoshita made up a thermos of coffee for the man and gave it to him. He's not the author's personal chauffeur, but works for a limo service that has a contract with Mr. Tamura to provide a car whenever he needs it. Mr. Tamura often asks for him to be his driver, and he's come to know him fairly well."

"Ah, so that's the kind of driver he is."

"It's quite a reputable limo company and as you can imagine the driver keeps things close to his chest. It takes more than coffee to get him to reveal anything. Though he did say that when Mr. Tamura goes out, he often takes someone from sales or an editor from his publishers with him to act as a kind of secretary for him."

How is that relevant? Otoha wondered.

"He's pompous, he bosses people around like they're his personal valet, ordering them to do this for him, do that for him, and he's universally disliked. And if they're not careful he makes the publisher pay for meals and the car service. He's so stingy, even though he could write off the car's service fees."

Kuroiwa said the driver didn't talk much, but he really did get him to open up, Otoha thought, impressed. What you'd expect of a former policeman.

"He said he was surprised that he didn't bring anybody from the publishers today. It must be something really important, or else something he doesn't want others to know about, he said."

"Makes sense," Otoha said.

They all nodded in agreement.

"At any rate, Mr. Shirakawa's collection seems to be important to him," Sasai murmured.

"But what's it all about, anyway?" Otoha said to herself, not expecting a reply.

"Beyond that I have no idea," Kuroiwa said, clapping Sasai on the shoulder. "That's probably your job, everyone."

"True enough."

"Just to play it safe, though," he added, "I'll be right outside the drawing room door."

"Yeah, good idea. Thanks."

They watched Detective Kuroiwa as he exited.

"I don't know how long this will take, but everyone should go back to their regular duties," Ako said. "Otoha and I will be sorting collections, and the rest of you get ready for patrons to come."

They all nodded slowly to each other and returned to their posts.

Otoha went with Ako to the collections sorting room and resumed the work she'd been doing the day before. She diligently stamped books while Ako updated their record books.

The only sounds in the room were of her stamping away, and Ako writing down memos and tapping in updates on the computer. It was a very tranquil time, which Otoha enjoyed.

When she suddenly looked up, she realized it had been an hour since they'd left Mr. Tamura and Masako back in the drawing room.

"What could be going on up there?" Ako said, noticing Otoha glancing at the clock on the wall.

"I hope he's not getting really upset at Masako."

"Well, she's not the type to let a little anger get her down."

The two of them chuckled.

"Have you and Masako known each other a long time?" Otoha asked.

"Uh-uh. We met here for the first time."

"Really? But you're so close I was sure you'd been friends for a while."

"No. See, Masako was on staff at a large library, while I just worked at a small bookstore near Shizuoka station."

"Is that so?" Otoha said.

"Masako's a hard worker, a real . . . career woman, would you say? While I worked at a tiny little store that sold cigarettes, newspapers, and stationery goods alongside books."

"Yeah, but selling all kinds of things like that you must have picked up on a lot about people in the neighborhood."

"Yes. Good point. This was back when there weren't convenience stores everywhere. So I learned which brands of smokes the men in the neighborhood preferred, what grades people's children were in, things like that. Plus their tastes in books, of course."

"Did you run the bookstore with your family?" Otoha asked.

"That's right!"

Okay—but by family *was it with your parents? Or your husband?* Otoha almost asked but stifled herself. That was going a bit too far, she decided. At any rate, the fact that Ako lived by herself in the dorm now must mean something had happened with the store, or to Ako.

Otoha had just taken a breath when the door to the

sorting room opened. She looked up in surprise to find Masako standing there. "Masako!"

"Are you okay?" Ako asked.

Masako gave a faint nod and motioned to them.

"Mr. Tamura said he wants everyone to gather in the drawing room."

"Eh?"

"Rest easy. He said he'd like to thank everyone."

Otoha exchanged a look with Ako. "Thank goodness," she said.

"I'll go gather the others. You two go to the drawing room."

When they entered the room Tamura was enthusiastically shaking Sasai's hand.

"Thank you! Thank you so, so much!" he said.

"No problem, you're, uh, welcome."

Tamura had grabbed Sasai's hands à la Western style and was vigorously shaking it up and down. Just like some politician's handshake, Otoha thought.

"I'd like to thank all of you as well," Tamura went on. "Please forgive me for acting so rudely." There were traces of tears on his cheeks.

A little rudeness Otoha could live with, but she could have done without the fiery, belligerent attitude. When Otoha saw how vigorously he was shaking Sasai's hand, she spontaneously edged back, trying to get behind Ako.

"I am really so, so grateful!"

Now he was facing them. As Otoha flinched, Ako said decisively, "Your words of thanks are quite enough, sir," and she stepped in between Tamura and Otoha. Her words were gentle yet made it crystal clear there would be no handshaking in their future.

"Really . . .?" Tamura said.

"No need for apologies. We were just doing our job . . . Really, don't worry about it."

At this point Minami, Tokai, and Tokuda all filed in. Tamura thanked them equally and bowed deeply.

He's not such a bad guy after all, Otoha thought. *For better or worse, though, he's just too intense. If he's going to show his true colors now, it would have been nice if he'd done so a little earlier.*

"Ah, so everyone's here now," Tamura said, gazing around the drawing room. "I'm truly sorry about today. I apologize for causing such a ruckus. I hope you'll see this as a reflection of my love for literature. It's easy enough to, uh, express my thanks, but as I've already told Mr. Sasai here, I'll also be helping support your efforts working at this library as well."

Tamura looked over at Sasai.

"I'm planning to donate my own collection to the library, of course, but I'm hoping you'll allow me to contribute a small monetary sum as well every year . . ."

Sasai, beside him, gave a small nod.

"Well, then, if there's anything else you'd like to know, please don't hesitate . . ."

"If you don't mind, could you tell us the reason you came here today?" Masako asked, gently, but firmly.

"Well, about that . . ."

"After you leave, Mr. Tamura, I think I need to give some sort of explanation. Since we were all a bit flustered by this today . . . But wouldn't it be better to hear it directly from you?"

"I suppose so . . ."

Tamura looked confused for a second, then pulled himself together. "I guess you're right," he said and began explaining.

"As I'm sure some of you are aware, Mr. Shirakawa was my one and only rival. As a young man he wrote some amazing works, and we used to get together to talk about work and novels . . . I truly envied him. I was jealous of his talent. Despite his great genius, though, he was such a kind and good person, and we spent countless hours drinking cheap liquor and talking. He was the only other writer I could open up with like that."

Tamura smiled, as if nostalgic for those bygone days.

"But some trivial thing came between us, and we parted ways. Since then, we've never gotten back in touch. Ever since then I was sure that he found me a fool, so I never reached out to him."

He exchanged a glance with Masako, gave a small nod, and continued.

"I came here today because I'd heard he'd donated his collection to you. I wanted to settle this once and for all for myself. I'd always had an inferiority complex toward him, and decided I had to stop thinking that he was far superior to me as a writer and that he had always looked down on me. I only sent him complimentary copies of my first couple of books, with an inscription in them. After our estrangement, I never sent any more. I decided that if there wasn't a single one of my novels in his collection, he was a small-minded person who hated me and had gotten rid of them."

"And . . . ?" Sasai asked, looking at Masako. She shook her head. *Let's let him tell the story? There weren't any?* Her gesture could have worked for either interpretation.

". . . and my books were there. *All* my books, not just the ones I gave him, but every single one I've ever published . . . He'd read them all."

Tamura burst into tears. He hid his face in his arm and briskly wiped away the tears.

"I've been so petty, so narrow-minded . . . and it makes me sad. Why? *Why* couldn't I have reached out to him again . . . ?"

Tamura's sobs rang out through the room for a while.

By the time Tamura had finished looking through Shirakawa's books, and gotten in his car and left, it was around 10:00 p.m.

After Tamura's car had driven through the gate, Sasai turned to them all. "Thank you, everyone," he said. "You all worked so hard today."

Otoha and the others thanked him, bowing to Sasai one after the other.

"Thanks for everything."

"You all must be so worn out."

"What a wild ride."

They all expressed their appreciation to each other.

"How about you all go have the staff dinner?" Sasai said. "I'll man the reception desk."

"No, we'll handle the reception tonight," Masako proposed. "Those of you who traveled to the warehouse should go eat first."

"No, I'm good. *You* two should be the ones who take a break," Sasai said, brushing aside the idea.

"Go and eat now, Mr. Sasai. We're all eating late this evening, and I imagine our chef Mr. Kinoshita's getting a bit irritated, waiting for us. I'll eat my bento later on."

With Ako urging them on even more, Sasai, Tokai, Tokuda, and Otoha decided to go have dinner.

"This is the first time I've seen Mr. Sasai have dinner with everyone," Tokai whispered to Otoha as they mounted the stairs to the second floor.

"Really?"

"It's a rare event, at any rate, since he always does things on his own."

"Because Masako and Ako urged him to?"

"That's part of it, but he must be really tired as well."

As Ako had predicted, Kinoshita was quite upset.

"Today's the day for *Mamaya* and I was wondering what to do if you didn't come and I had too much food . . . You should have eaten it earlier when the rice was freshly made."

"Mamaya . . . ?"

Otoha wanted to know what kind of dish it was, but Kinoshita disappeared back into the kitchen.

The four of them sat down at a table, and as they looked at each other Otoha felt like she'd come to an izakaya. But this was different from a drinking party, for no one here spoke up. Sasai's face across from her looked quite pale and she was sure hers might look the same.

"Well, here you go."

Kinoshita brought over several trays, placing one in front of each of them. Each had soup, a main dish, and—orange-colored rice?

"What is this?"

"It's carrot rice! With unlimited second helpings!"

Sure enough, the rice was packed full of so many carrots, that's all you could see.

Otoha started with the soup, which was a potage with roughly mashed potatoes. Not very showy, yet the wonderful flavor spread throughout her. She let out a deep sigh. Not the type of sigh she'd let out in front of Mr. Tamura, but one of deep satisfaction nonetheless.

She next turned to the carrot rice.

"Wow . . . this is delicious," she said as she took a big bite. The sweetness of carrots, the aroma of soy sauce—what a gentle, delicious flavor the rice had.

"*Mamaya* was the name of a restaurant that the author Kuniko Mukoda opened for her sister," Sasai explained as he enjoyed the carrot rice.

He'd taken a very small bite with his chopsticks and was chewing. His mouth and face hardly moved at all, his expression unchanged. He was more neat and tidy than classy.

"Is that so?"

"Ms. Higuchi, have you read any of Kuniko Mukoda's books . . .?"

"Just a few of her essays. I'm not so good with plays and scenarios . . . Her essays were wonderful and I wanted to read more but just didn't have the chance."

"I can imagine someone working in a bookstore dealing with new books all the time might not." Tokai nodded as if it couldn't be helped.

"New books I want to read, and ones I had to read

for work, just kept coming out." She didn't mean to sound like she was justifying herself, but it did.

"But boy this tastes so great, no matter how often I have it," Tokuda murmured.

"It sure does. It's so tasty it's hard to believe that rice tastes like this with just carrots and fried tofu."

"It's healthy too," Tokuda added.

"Good for when you're tired," said Tokai.

The main dishes were lotus root cooked in soy and chili pepper, and the head and bony parts of yellowtail cooked in soy sauce and sweet sake. Both were mildly seasoned and went well with the rice.

As they were talking, Kinoshita came over.

"Seems like you had to deal with a tough customer, didn't you," he said, smiling wryly.

"I heard he came here and said all kinds of things, too," Sasai said. "Sorry to have troubled you," he added.

"That guy . . . He railed against us, saying, *You're a cafe that features a menu taken from books, so how come you don't have* this? *How come you don't have* that?"

"He did?" Sasai asked.

"Maybe he didn't like it that the menu didn't include any dishes from *his* books."

"I see."

"*How come it's all old books, old authors?*" he complained. "*Nobody reads those.*"

"Such an impolite person. Well, if he'd been a customer back when I worked in the coffee shop I would have run him out," Kinoshita muttered. "Things are different now, so I put up with it."

"I'm really sorry you had to go through that," Sasai said, getting to his feet and apologizing.

"It's okay, it's okay. You don't need to apologize. Actually," Kinoshita said, "what I was thinking was . . . You're all pretty worn out today, right? The library will close up in an hour . . . and I have a wonderful microbrew in stock. How about you all having a glass?"

He smiled like a mischievous child.

Taken by surprise, Tokai looked at Sasai.

"Did you know," Kinoshita went on, "that the concept behind the restaurant Mamaya was for women to come in by themselves and have a drink? They'd eat cooked lotus root and a meat and potato stew, and finish off with a bite of curry rice. That's the kind of place it was."

"No kidding?"

"Back then it was hard for a woman to feel comfortable going into a restaurant alone, especially if she wanted a drink, which means that if we're to truly re-create the experience you need to have some liquor."

They all looked over at Sasai.

"Sounds good." He was smiling wryly. "I won't have any . . . I don't drink that much. But today was hard on everyone, so why not, occasionally."

"Yay!"

"Thank you so much."

Kinoshita came out with the microbrew beer he'd been saving up special, in small brown-colored bottles with fancy labels.

He brought over three glasses and poured out the beer for them.

"At the bottom of the menu," Otoha said, "it says you have all sorts of microbrews at market prices, and I was wondering about that."

"Well, it's a night library. It'd be quite a shame if the cafe didn't at least have beer."

"Makes sense."

"This microbrew was made by young women who work at a sake maker over on the Japan Sea coast side and decided to try making their own liquor. They've only been making it for a few years but it's quite tasty."

"Really? Brewed by women, huh?" Otoha said.

"It's slightly acidic and goes really well with the carrot rice, I think."

The beer was a light brown color, slightly cloudy, without much foam.

"Cheers!" Otoha said.

Otoha took a deep drink and found it refreshing, but with a slight bitterness and acidity.

"This really hits home," Tokai groaned.

"It really does. It's delicious."

Kinoshita nodded. "You're all tired out today, so you deserve a treat."

"I think I'll have a glass myself, after all," Sasai murmured.

"But you don't drink, Mr. Sasai," said Kinoshita.

"I don't drink very *much*, I said. It's not like I don't drink at all."

"Now you're talking!"

Kinoshita went out to get a beer and a glass.

"Man, today was exhausting," Tokai said, the first to drain his glass. "That writer really upset me."

"I know," Otoha agreed.

"But . . . it didn't feel so bad in the end."

"True enough . . ." Sasai nodded deeply. "When I saw him break into tears, I thought that this is a pretty nice job to have."

"Yeah."

"This job exists for times like these. I think the owner created this place for these kinds of situations."

An old library . . . a library devoted just to writers' collections . . . definitely a most odd, unconventional sort of place.

"I don't know how long we can keep it going here . . . but let's go on doing our best."

Sasai had not yet taken a sip, yet the corners of his eyes were already red.

EPISODE THREE

ANNE OF GREEN GABLES' BREAD AND BUTTER AND CUCUMBERS

A month had passed since Otoha Higuchi had come to the Night Library.

She'd been so busy, the time seemed to have just flown by. Yet each and every thing she'd done in the meantime—talking with Ako and Masako while they worked together, eating dinner with Tokuda and the others, watching movies with some of her colleagues in Minami's dorm room—had all seemed so special, so meaningful, that it felt like she'd been here for—well, years.

The streamed film they watched together with Ako and Masako was *Little Women*, entitled *Story of My Life* in Japanese. They'd all read *Little Women* and its sequel, of course, and as they watched the film they picked it apart: "This part isn't like the novel," one of them said. "Those lines weren't in the original, were they?" another piped in.

"Still, this might be the best film adaptation of *Little Women*." Despite all her sharp criticisms as they'd watched it, after it ended, Masako still praised the film.

Masako brought coffee that day, and Ako a homemade apple cake. Minami had provided her room to watch, so they told her she didn't need to make anything. *Don't you worry about it, either*, they told Otoha, but she said she wanted to buy some potato chips. Her firm belief was you gotta have potato chips when you watch a movie.

Masako and Ako had so briskly decided the division of duties that Otoha was sure they were quite used to these girls' days out. Not just this kind of gathering, but they seemed to be veterans of all sorts of get-togethers—mothers' groups, relatives. That's how neatly they'd divided up the roles.

"You say this is the best one, but what you're comparing it to, Masako, is that other one where Elizabeth Taylor plays Amy." Ako laughed.

"Are those two the only film versions?" Masako asked.

"Yes. But I agree that the free adaption they made of the sequel to *Little Women* in this version is much better than that earlier one."

"I remember how I felt as a child, when I first read

EPISODE THREE

Little Women. When Jo and Laurie couldn't marry it made me so sad. I wanted them to get married so badly."

"I know!"

Otoha and Minami both chimed in as well.

"We knew they loved each other, so why don't they marry?" Masako went on. ". . . I couldn't understand their feelings. And I don't understand, too, how in the sequel Jo chooses that other man."

"I know what you mean, but this version kind of convinced me."

"I know, me too. But it still hurts. I feel like I did when I was a child." As she said this, Masako grew teary-eyed, which caught Otoha off guard. Masako always seemed so pragmatic, and this was an unexpected side of her.

"How about watching the film of *Anne of Green Gables* next?" Minami suggested after they'd chatted a while.

"I've seen a film of *Anne of Green Gables*, but is this one different?" Masako asked.

"Well . . . the film was made in 2015 . . ." Minami said as she checked her cell phone.

"No, I saw a much earlier one," Masako said. "It was wonderful."

"Do you mean the 1985 version . . .?" Minami asked.

"Right . . . that's about the right time period."

"That's this one. I remember seeing it in a theater, and that scene where Anne appears and is waiting in the station for Matthew—that really got to me. I couldn't stop crying after that. I mean, it was exactly Anne's world as I'd pictured it. It was a wonderful film."

Otoha remembered how, when she'd first showed up at the library with her wobbly suitcase Sasai had remarked "Are you Anne of Green Gables?"

She'd been surprised by that and couldn't respond well, but deep down she'd thought, *This person might well become my confidant.* It made her feel a bit relieved. Soon after that she realized there were lots of confidants like that here in the library, people who'd read the same books as her, who'd experienced the same sort of adolescence. Among the staff members, as well as some of the library's users.

"I'm sure that's wonderful, but so is the more recent adaptation. I know you'll like it. You should check it out sometime."

"Okay, then that will be our film next month," they decided, and their gathering ended.

Other times, Otoha met with some of her old friends.

Mana Sato, a childhood friend, worked for a company in Ote-machi in Tokyo and came all the way out to the library by train and bus to see her.

"Wow, this is a nicer place than I was expecting," Mana said as she came into Otoha's room and looked around.

"Nicer place . . .? What kind of place did you think I was living in?!"

Otoha asked this as she poured Mana some coffee from a pot that Masako had brewed. The day before, Otoha happened to mention that her friend was coming to visit and that she had no good cups to use, and Masako had said, "I'll bring some over. No need to thank me," and had brought over both the coffee and some mugs.

"This coffee is delicious," Mana said as she sipped it, and Otoha explained how Masako had made it for her.

"So your workplace is quite decent after all."

"What sort of place did you expect me to be working in?" Otoha asked.

"Your mother told my mom you were working in some night trade live-in, and she kept on crying and crying, so I was sure you were working in some kind of sketchy place."

"Sketchy? No way."

"Back home if you say it's a live-in deal people think it must be a pachinko parlor, and add to that the idea of night work, well . . ."

"But I *told* her I was working in a library."

"I don't think she believed you."

Otoha let out a deep sigh.

"Your mother's very worried about you," Mana said. "You'll have to put her mind at ease."

"How?"

"Invite her here. Have her tour Tokyo."

"How's she going to tour Tokyo here? We're out in the countryside."

They looked at each other and burst out laughing.

"Well, if she can't tour Tokyo at least she can tour the library."

"I suppose . . ."

But after considering what Mana had told her, she knew it wouldn't be easy to simply invite her mother to "come visit me."

"Be a dutiful child. You're their only daughter after all."

"That applies to you, too, Mana."

After Mana had graduated from a college in their region, she was hired by a trading firm in Tokyo. In Otoha's hometown going to work in the big city made her one of the elite, which in turn permitted her to insist on some old-fashioned view like being a *dutiful child*.

"Next time you have to come over to *my* place," Mana said.

Hers wasn't a live-in arrangement, but a nice apartment she rented on her own.

"I'm afraid Tokyo is beyond me, and most humbly I must say I find it hard to go there," Otoha said, her words overblown.

She'd said it as a joke, but truthfully she did feel a sense of inferiority.

"What're you talking about? What kind of place do you think Kinshicho is, where I live? Come and visit and you'll see. And my place is not much bigger than yours."

As they talked Otoha relaxed more, and she wound up promising to visit Mana the following month.

THE NEXT DAY, AS Otoha was working with Masako and Ako in the collections sorting room Sasai came in.

"Sorry to bother you, but someone found this book," he said.

He was holding a paperback book.

"What is it?"

Masako and Ako were at their desks, typing in data into the computers. Otoha was unpacking newly donated books, taking them from cardboard boxes and stacking them up beside the women.

The three of them studied the book he was holding.

"What's the problem with it?"

"Take a look at this," Sasai said.

When he opened up the back cover of the paperback, the three of them reacted the same. "Oh, my gosh!"

There was nothing there. Just a blank page.

"What about the collections stamp?" Masako asked, flustered.

"That's the problem. There isn't any," Sasai said.

"Where was the book?"

"A patron just brought it over now. He found it somewhere on the first floor and looked all over trying to find where it had come from, but in the end couldn't figure it out. When he tried to return it to the shelves, he noticed it didn't have a collections stamp."

"And that patron . . .?"

"He's already gone. He just reported to reception—about finding it on the first floor without a stamp in it—and then he left. Ms. Enokida said she was so surprised she forgot to ask anything more."

"Goodness."

"But it was definitely on the first floor."

"How could that happen? How could there not be a collections stamp in it?" Otoha asked, looking at each of them.

"I have no clue," Ako replied. "Maybe we simply forgot to stamp it."

"But different people check it at each of three stages—when the book's stamped, when it's catalogued, and when it's placed on the shelves." Sasai looked baffled. "I doubt anyone would forget to."

"Well, people *are* fallible," Ako said, not sounding overly confident about it.

"And we do a yearly sorting of the library's holdings," added Sasai.

"Maybe it's a book that's been here less than a year," Masako said, as if to herself.

"You're saying it's fairly new, then?" Sasai asked her.

"Right."

"Well, one other possibility, one I'd rather not contemplate, is that someone stole a book from the collection and substituted this copy . . ."

"I guess that's possible," Masako said, nodding.

"For the undiscerning, what we have here are just a bunch of old books," Sasai said, "but for fans, they're priceless."

"True enough," Otoha said, nodded, and then with a start noticed something. "But you can't take books out of here, can you? If you're carrying a book and take one step outside, the alarm will ring . . . There's a large sign that says that at the entrance."

Sasai, Masako, and Ako exchanged a glance, an embarrassed look on their faces.

"You haven't told Otoha yet?" Ako asked.

"Well, no. I wasn't hiding it or anything, but I simply forgot to," Masako said.

"What are you talking about?" Otoha asked.

"Actually, that's not true."

"No way!" Otoha exclaimed.

"I mean we just stamp the books and put them on the shelves, right? We don't put the kind of laminated magnetic strips inside like other libraries do these days."

"That's true."

"If we do all sorts of extra things it'll damage the

appearance of the books . . . the owner won't like that and will say you won't be able to appreciate the way the books were when the authors owned them."

"Plus there's the added time, effort, and cost," Sasai said, ever the pragmatist.

"I thought it was odd, too," Otoha said. "I wondered how you controlled them without those."

"So anyway, we decided to put out that sign and remind people over and over at the entrance again about the policy. We'll have our very own *library detective* check it out and if the thefts continue, consider other ways of handling it."

"So that's the way it is . . ."

Otoha was a bit shocked at not being informed before about the setup, though it all made perfect sense.

"Anyway, our first priority is to figure out why this book is here, isn't it," Otoha said.

"But it might be going too far to think it was stolen. If someone's stolen it, wouldn't they just take it? Why replace it with another copy? I don't get it." Ako said this as she studied the book. "And most people wouldn't think it's possible to just take a book out. Which means one possibility is it's someone who knows it's okay to . . ." Ako stopped before she finished and shook her head. She probably didn't want to suspect any of the people here with her.

"But if another volume has been substituted on the shelves it makes it hard to notice the original missing," said Otoha.

"But we'd still notice when we did a collections sorting and other checks."

"But only a small group of people would know that," Otoha said. "Just the people who work here."

"At any rate we need to start checking."

"First we need to go through our holdings," Ako said. "Find out how many copies of this book we have and which one is missing."

Otoha looked at the book's cover. It was the novel *Schoolgirl* by Osamu Dazai.

"I think . . . we'll have lots of copies of this book," she said.

"It's no exaggeration to say that most authors have read it," Ako said.

"Then start with authors from the beginning of the alphabet and check each and every one. We can search the intranet for authors that have it listed and search these collections one by one." Sasai looked over at Otoha. "Can you and Masako take care of this?"

"I can do it on my own," Otoha said.

"You could, but it would be better to have two of you checking it, just to be sure."

"Understood."

"And I'll get in touch with our detective, Mr. Kuroiwa, and see what he has to say. If necessary I'll have him join us."

"Thank you for doing that," Otoha said.

Otoha and Masako went up to the second floor together.

I CAN'T READ BOOKS.

This thought ran through my mind as, next to Otoha, I checked every copy of Dazai's *Schoolgirl*.

Laptop in one hand, Otoha checked which authors had a copy of the novel, and would call out, for instance, "Next is Natsuo Ayukawa," and I would simply take that volume down from the stacks. It must be hard to do this job with a laptop in one hand, and I told her several times I'd switch places, but Otoha only smiled and said, "I'm good!" In times like these it really helped that she volunteered to take on the heavier tasks. I'm so happy such a good person has joined us.

As these grateful thoughts came to me, another part of my mind held a different thought.

I can't read books.

Not just at times like this when I'm working.

I can't after I get up in the morning, when I make coffee, when I'm drinking it, when I'm here talking with these young people and burst out laughing.

I can't read books. I can't read books. I can't read them anymore. It's been that way for a long time.

I never forgot this, not for a moment.

Those simple times when you get lost in a book, so focused you don't hear any sound around you, you're taken to another world, and several hours later when you finish reading, you experience that lonely, yet fulfilling moment when you feel cast out from the world.

I can never enjoy that again.

It's not that I can't read. I can. I can read and understand. It's just that, unlike in the past, I can no longer give myself over to reading the way I used to, totally, body and soul. Even when I do try reading I can't make it past the first few pages.

Somehow, over a few days, I might be able to make it through a book. But the joy is gone. All I feel is fatigue. And later just relief at being able, if I try hard, to read anything at all.

It was when I turned sixty that this began. About ten years ago.

At first I didn't acknowledge it. Or maybe I should say I didn't notice it.

I was a librarian for many years, and though a library is piled high with books, that didn't mean I didn't buy my own. Actually, I bought more than other people. There were lots of books I wanted to have nearby, and I bought and read a considerable number of newly published ones. I liked rereading books, too, that I particularly enjoyed.

But then I began to notice that unread books were piling up around me at home. I'd go to bookstores, hear about books from people and TV and want them and buy them right away. But after reading a few pages I'd toss them aside and the pile of unread books in my room only grew.

I'm just tired, I don't have the time, I'm too busy—these were my thoughts. But after some years passed, I had to admit it to myself.

Something is off. Something's happened that hasn't before. I might've thought, if only I had some free time I could read again sometime, but that wasn't the case.

The fact is I can't read books.

MASAKO WAS BORN IN one of the older downtown districts of Tokyo. Her father was an ordinary employee, her mother a full-time housewife. She had an older brother and younger sister. Her older brother went to a prestigious national university while she and her sister just attended junior colleges. Masako's grades were good enough for her to go to a four-year college, but at the time going to a junior college was par for the course for young women. She felt thankful just to be able to go to one. She got certified as a librarian, took the licensing exam and found a job. The place she worked at was a public library in Tokyo, and she was hired as a librarian, a proper city employee. But as was common for women then, she and others around her saw it as a place-holder job, the expectation being that she would quit to get married in a few years, at the latest before she turned thirty.

Her father was straitlaced and domineering at home, though not one prone to the kind of violent behavior or physical abuse you see in the news so much these days. At dinner he'd always insist on one extra dish to go along with his drinks, sashimi or grilled fish or something, and no one could ever talk back to him, but that was the extent of it. A man of few words, not good at expressing his feelings to his children, yet on holidays he'd take them to amusement parks, shopping centers, or hot springs resorts. For someone of that period he was an indulgent father.

Yet right around the time Masako got her job, her father had an affair. The woman was someone he met at a bar, and the whole thing came out because he kept frequenting her place and not coming home. The affair in itself was surprising, but what really came as a shock was when her parents, both nearly sixty, got divorced. She'd thought, baselessly, that even if her father had an affair her mother would put up with it. But in about a year they were divorced. Her father had insisted he wanted a divorce, and for some reason her mother didn't oppose it that much.

So it seemed, at least . . . so it seemed. The two of them confined their discussions about it to themselves, with the children only hearing they were getting divorced later on.

At the time her older brother was working for the city office and was married and had been assigned to a regional office. Naturally Masako and her sister lived with their mother, and her brother continued to be assigned to one regional office after another. Her brother also had children, so instead of their mother living with him as you might expect, Masako continued to live with her until she passed away at seventy.

Masako looked after her mother, helped her younger sister finish junior college and get married, and by the time she realized it she'd missed her own timing to get married. Her brother helped them out a little financially, but she didn't expect anything beyond that mainly because her mother disliked any help. Her mother was embarrassed by the divorce, and had an inferiority complex concerning her son, his wife, and his wife's family. She herself hadn't been the cause of what happened with Masako's father, yet she felt ashamed of herself because of it. She may well have quickly consented to the divorce because she felt humiliated to have lost her husband's affections. Understanding those feelings, Masako found it hard to ask her brother for any more support.

After her mother passed away, it was up to Masako to care for her aging father, after he'd broken up with the other woman. She thought it was all quite absurd, but she was resigned to it since there was no one else to take on the task. She was happy, at least, that she didn't have to quit her job.

As he was near death, her father muttered, "I wish your mother had been a little more against it back then." *He must mean the divorce*, she figured, but pretended not to have heard. *What a selfish thing to say*, she thought, dismayed.

The library Masako worked at was one of the flagship libraries of Tokyo. When she was hired, computers had yet to be introduced, and books were organized and catalogued using paper cards.

What Masako was assigned to and spent most of her life doing—heading up the section at the end—was that of "adviser," namely the head of the reference section.

At their peak, twenty staff members were assigned to the reference section, their job from morning till night to answer users' questions. The main two ways were via phone calls and face-to-face at the reference desk.

There were all sorts of questions; for instance someone would call in, mutter a line from a poem and ask, "Who's the author of that?" or "Are there any books about how in the Edo period they handled birth control in the red light district?" or "What day of the week was May 10, 1924, and what was the weather like?" or "Do you have a copy there of last year's economic white paper?"

Nowadays the internet would provide all the answers, the massive amounts of questions coming into the library something you could now easily google. On the busiest days they had a hundred inquiries at the reference desk, and two hundred over the phone. At the end of the day, she was so exhausted her brain felt numb.

From the mid-1980s computer systems were gradually introduced, with information being organized digitally. But the height of Masako's career was in this transition period, so she swam through the sea of data using both library cards and computers.

When she was first hired at the library, a veteran librarian told her, "A person can remember, say, 5,000 volumes. But a person here has to remember 10,000." Meaning, when a user asked where a certain book was, she had to be able to instantly point to the right place.

She worked frantically, memorized frantically, and read books frantically.

And when she finally thought she'd be able to read at her leisure, enjoy it just for herself . . . Masako lost the joy of reading.

EPISODE THREE 131

A little while back, when the author Junichiro Tamura had insisted on seeing Tadasuke Shirakawa's collection of books, it was no lie when she said she'd read Shirakawa's work. Shirakawa was not a prolific writer, merely publishing a novella of maybe one hundred pages once a year in a literary magazine, and whenever these came out, she savored them. Even so, though, she never had the excited feeling she used to have.

She glanced at the title of one of Dazai's most famous novels next to *Schoolgirl* on the shelves. *No Longer Human*. In her case it was *No Longer a Reader*.

"Masako? How about it? Is it there?" Otoha asked and Masako snapped back to earth.

"Mr. Ayukawa's copy of *Schoolgirl* is here," Masako said, checking that there was a collections stamp on the inside back cover.

"Good. Let's move on . . . You know, I was thinking . . ." Otoha ventured hesitantly. "Is it really okay just to check this book, *Schoolgirl*?"

"What do you mean?"

"If you stole someone's book and substituted this one, in a sense it's easy— No, that's not it, if the book's about the same thickness and by the same author, and you put it there thinking no one will notice, then we need to check all of Osamu Dazai's paperbacks."

"I see . . ."

"And what's even scarier is the possibility it's not just Dazai. Stealing something from here and sticking in another substitute book . . ."

"But it might be that we simply forgot to stamp it, or a simple prank, perhaps."

"That's true. I was thinking maybe it's not anything malicious, but just a mistake."

"Or like when you bring a book with you from home in your bag, thinking you'll read it, and you see a different book here and take it home by mistake . . ."

"You know, that occurred to me too. If you're stealing it, you just pick it up and figure a way of getting it out of here."

Bags were all examined when people left the library. But this only involved the detective, Kuroiwa, or Ms. Kitazato from the front desk opening the bag and glancing inside. So if someone seriously wanted to steal a book, they could always hide it in under their clothes, which meant there was no guarantee a book would never be stolen.

There was, however, the room devoted to famous authors. That was another story. The place that housed the books donated by Ryoichi Kaito a few years ago, which originally gave the library its acclaim, was strictly guarded, and no one was allowed to bring in bags or coats. And like in an art museum, a staff member was always seated there, which made swiping a book from there no easy task.

"But I think that room with famous authors' books is more likely to be suspect than here. Here if you steal one and don't stick in a substitute, the chances are no one will notice, so there's no need to do something so elaborate."

"I'd say so," Otoha said.

"That said, we still need to check them."

"To what extent?"

"Well, *Schoolgirl* at this point."

Otoha nodded and went back to her task.

When was that? Masako wondered. When she heard that the amount of information a person is exposed to in a week nowadays is equal to the amount a person in the Victorian age was exposed to in their entire lifetime? The way this is expressed always changed. The amount of information in a day now is equal to a year's worth back in the Edo period, or a lifetime's worth in the Heian period, and so on . . .

If so, then you didn't need a huge amount of information to write an outstanding novel. No—it's kind of arrogant for people nowadays to think that the amount of information Murasaki Shikibu, author of *The Tale of Genji*, had a thousand years ago was a lot less than that of people today. Shikibu and her cohorts no doubt read extensively in Chinese literature, passing along all sorts of gossip, too, about what various figures at court were up to, what kind of poem someone had composed recently, and so on . . .

Who was it who'd told her about the amount of information people had? Ah, that's right—it had been him. The man who'd come nearly every week to the library . . .

At first, he'd phoned in questions. Asking about books that surveyed prewar household accounts. He was extremely impatient, and when Masako had asked him if he'd checked with the Diet Library, he shot back, "Of course I have. They didn't have it, so that's why I'm asking." His abrupt manner made her angry, but as calmly as she could, she told him about the materials they did have in their collection. The man gradually calmed down and at the end thanked her.

The following day he showed up in person at the reference desk and asked for her, wanting to thank her in person. He apologized for his rudeness over the phone, explaining how his professor had tasked him with collecting information and how flustered he'd been. He was a young researcher in sociology.

After that, he came many times to the reference desk, and she helped him each time. When Masako seemed busy he didn't stop by, but when she had a free moment he would, looking happy to see her. His blue shirt was a bit frayed at the sleeves but always neatly ironed, and she found him clean-cut and presentable.

Once he asked her, "Would you like to go out for a coffee?" Or more like, "I'd like to buy you a coffee to thank you." After some thought she'd said, "Sorry, but I can't. I have to work." And he stopped coming to the library.

I remember this sometimes, Masako thought. *If only I had gone for coffee with him, then maybe my life would have changed?*

When they had been searching the stacks together, it was the coffee man who'd told her about the amount of information people take in.

A year after the coffee man had abruptly stopped coming, he suddenly showed up one day, which made her quite happy. And then . . .

"I've been made associate professor," he said. "All thanks to you." She was thrilled, and got a lump in her throat, but all she managed to say was "Congratulations."

If only then she'd said, "How about going out for a coffee to celebrate?"

She thought about this over and over. Over and over, year after year.

This was Masako's second regret in her life. The second coffee. The coffee that she didn't drink. Perhaps this why she became so fond of coffee.

This happened around the time she was about to retire from the library. She finally decided to join an online thread, "Channel 2," that was all about libraries. Staff members of libraries contributed to it, and the conversations were for the most part fairly staid and collected. The fact that it was the middle of the night, and she lived in a hushed, sparsely populated area, had something to do with her decision to open up.

She wrote about how she couldn't read books anymore, her fears that someone like her wasn't fit for being a librarian, about her anxiety about her life once she stepped down from the library . . . and after she did, she received an odd reply.

> Greetings. My username is Seven Rainbows. I read your online responses about books and was quite struck by what you said. I have a job I would like you to help with. If you'd like, please get in touch with me.

The address given there was a temporary one: it would, according to this person, "Disappear at the end of the night."

She was always so cautious back then, Masako remembered, and even now she had no idea why she went ahead and responded to this sketchy sort of message, and had a Skype interview, and then accepted the job that he (or perhaps she) was offering.

"Masako, I don't see any book that isn't here," Otoha murmured, and which caught her by surprise.

I don't see any book that isn't here . . . what a strange paradoxical statement.

"Well, I guess we need to go to where the famous authors' books are," Masako said, crouched down in front of the shelves. "The security's tight there, so I doubt anything's been stolen. And the user who turned in the book said they'd found it on the first floor."

"I agree, but it's still best to go look."

The famous authors' room was a special space, made when Junichi Kaito's books were donated to the library.

Originally the room for Kaito's books was in a corner on the first floor, set apart from other authors' books, which were lined up on shelves in alphabetical order by last name. After this, bit by bit, they received more books from other well-known authors, which they then consolidated and moved en masse to a large room on the second floor, with a staff member always stationed at the door.

"I was wondering," Otoha asked, "what's the difference between the ordinary writers' works on the shelves and the ones kept in the famous writers' room? What differentiates the two?"

"I think it's mainly whether or not they've won literary prizes, but popularity and actual sales also play a part. Mr. Sasai generally decides which authors are put in that room. I imagine he consults with the owner to decide. That doesn't seem to have caused any problems so far, and no users have complained about it or anything, so I'd say their judgment so far has been spot on."

Masako had casually mentioned the word *owner* and so Otoha followed suit.

"But Mr. Sasai told me he's never met the owner," she said.

"Maybe he hasn't, but perhaps they talk on the phone or email each other?"

"Ah, that makes sense."

Then, a little hesitantly, Otoha ventured, "You've never met the owner either, Masako?"

"No."

Her reply seemed a bit too quick, Otoha thought. If this were a mystery novel, the chances were high she was lying . . . but would Masako do that?

"When I joined the staff I got emails, and we talked on Skype."

"Same with me," Otoha said, "though I used Zoom. So you know how to use Skype?"

"Of course. In my previous library I worked with the internet. I'm faster than most people with computers."

"Wow."

"Ha-ha! Young people seem so sure that older people are computer illiterates."

"Sorry!" Otoha bowed her head as they made their way up the stairs.

"I'm just kidding," Masako said.

On the second floor they entered a room on the opposite end from the dining hall and the drawing room.

Tokuda was seated at the entrance to the famous authors' room.

"Hello, Masako, Ms. Higuchi."

"We came to investigate Dazai's works . . ."

"I heard. I looked into them myself, actually . . ."

Tokuda gazed around the room. "As of now, there aren't any Dazai books that aren't here."

"I see . . . Could the two of us check one more time?"

Otoha thought Tokuda looked a bit put out. Lips tightened, he looked about to respond. But perhaps because it was Masako asking he didn't.

"With something like this it's best to have multiple checks. It's not that we don't trust you, Mr. Tokuda. Sorry." Masako smiled as she apologized to him.

"Of course. I understand."

"We'll go ahead and check, then."

Otoha and Masako examined every last one of the authors whose collections contained Dazai books, but nothing was missing.

"There really aren't any missing," Masako said.

"Right?" Tokuda said proudly.

Perhaps because there were no visitors, Tokuda shadowed them closely the whole time. Honestly, Otoha felt it a little *oppressive*, a little annoying.

"Well done, Mr. Tokuda." Masako turned around so abruptly to praise him he was taken by surprise, perhaps, and couldn't help but smile.

Masako is really something, Otoha thought, impressed. Knowing just how to deal with the touchy Tokuda . . .

"So, what's next?" Masako murmured as they exited the famous authors' room. "For now let's go report to Mr. Sasai that we didn't find any copies of *Schoolgirl* missing."

"Okay."

IN THE END, SASAI and Masako talked it over and decided to keep the copy of *Schoolgirl* behind the reception desk for a while in the Lost and Found box.

After the search for *Schoolgirl*, Otoha went to the dining hall.

"What's today's menu?" she asked as she took a seat. She was there at a different time from the others, so she sat by herself at the counter.

"Tonight's *Anne of Green Gables* night," Kinoshita said.

"That sounds wonderful! Are there really that many places in *Anne of Green Gables* where food is mentioned?" Otoha tilted her head, considering it. "I know there's the part where she mistakes pain medicine for vanilla extract and puts it in a layer cake with a layer of jam, and the scene where Diana takes a raspberry pie to school, right? What I recall are lots of images of sweets."

Kinoshita popped back into the kitchen and quickly returned with a flat white plate of sandwiches. He placed it in front of Otoha.

"Sandwiches?"

Ordinary ones, by the look of them. Refined in a way, with the crusts neatly trimmed off.

"Yep, that's what they are. I was told to make something from the *Anne of Green Gables* series of books, and I had to read *Anne of Green Gables*, *Anne of Avonlea*, and *Anne of the Island* to figure out a menu. And the owner also sent me a ton of cookbooks based on the series."

"No kidding."

"*Anne of Green Gables Recipe Notebook, Anne of Green Gables Cookbook, Encyclopedia of Anne of Green Gables' Life, The World of Anne of Green Gables* . . . besides the original novels I think I must have read six or seven other related books."

"Wow," Otoha said, impressed.

"A lot of work, let me tell you. And yet I couldn't find the kind of dish I was looking for. It was all very simple recipes—roast chicken, salted pork cooked with vegetables, lettuce salad . . . And the novels never said how these were prepared."

"So what did you do?"

"There was this weird scene in *Anne of Avonlea*. Do you know it? A famous writer was supposed to visit

Anne's home and they all make a sumptuous meal for him but he never shows up . . ."

"Yes, I remember that!" Otoha said. "The food gets all squished, and the plate they borrowed from someone gets broken."

"Right, that's it. So they go to another person's home, someone who has the same kind of plate, hoping to buy one, but that person isn't at home . . ."

"It gets even worse," Otoha said,

"Right. The owner comes back, makes tea for them and says, 'I'm sorry I only have bread, butter, and cucumbers,' but Anne and Diana are so starving that the bread, butter, and cucumbers taste delicious. And it really does sound delicious. I don't know that much about *Anne of Green Gables*, or about novels in general, but that scene really stands out for me, the way it describes how wonderful the food tasted . . . Especially the way it describes the joy of eating."

"You may well be right."

"I thought about this a lot and I believe that the cucumbers mentioned may have been pickled. Though other translations of the book only say it's bread, butter, and cucumbers. But I can't picture them crunching on fresh cucumbers . . . So anyway, that's how I came up with my own version, which is this. Bread, butter, and fresh cucumber sandwiches. That seemed a bit inadequate, though, so I also made roast chicken sandwiches. I think they must have eaten those as well. Please, go ahead."

"Thank you. I can't wait," Otoha said.

There was something green between slices of soft bread. Otoha took a bite and sure enough the blend of cucumbers and butter leaped out into her mouth, with a simple, yet deep taste.

"Mr. Kinoshita, this is really delicious! It's hard to believe the ingredients are that simple."

"Thanks. I just sliced the cucumbers very thin and rubbed them with salt."

Otoha tried the roast chicken sandwich next.

"This is wonderful too. The chicken is so moist."

"I simply added salt and pepper to the chicken breasts as I roasted them, and then a little French dressing before I put it in the sandwich."

"They're all very simple flavors. You can really savor all the ingredients."

"I think that's how things were back in those times. Plus, I don't think Montgomery, a pastor's wife, would like writing long descriptions of how food tasted."

"That makes sense."

On top of the flat plate of sandwiches was a small dish with green peas.

Otoha tried them and found them softly boiled, with a taste of butter.

"Those are green peas sautéed in butter. I finished them by adding a spoonful of sugar. Do you remember how, when they invited Mrs. Morgan to Green Gables, Anne added too much sugar and spoiled the peas?"

"You've read the books very closely, Mr. Kinoshita. Much more than I have."

"No, just the parts about food. I pored over those to come up with a menu."

As always, he served her coffee after the meal, along with a side dish. Brown, slightly large cubes.

"Mr. Kinoshita, this is . . .?"

"Chocolate caramel."

"Really? Anne's chocolate caramel? The kind she always wanted to eat?"

"That's right."

"Ever since I was little I've always been curious about what that tasted like. Whenever I eat Morinaga brand Chocoballs, I wonder if that's how her chocolate caramels tasted."

Otoha took one of the chocolate-colored squares and popped it into her mouth. It melted in her mouth, with a thick aftertaste of both chocolate and caramel. A taste similar to the kind of fresh caramel chocolates that were popular here a while ago, but with a pleasant aroma of milk.

"This is so good!"

Otoha couldn't help turning to Mr. Kinoshita.

"Mr. Kinoshita, let's market this! Right here! We'll call it Anne of Green Gables' Chocolate Caramel! Sell it online too! People will *love* it!"

"No thanks. Do you know how much work goes into making it? I came an hour earlier than usual today and spent the whole time stirring the pot." He made a stirring motion.

"It's that much trouble to make?"

"It's not easy, believe me."

"Please make it again sometime," Otoha said.

"You like it that much?"

"I really do."

Kinoshita placed three more squares on her plate.

"Wow, thank you. I'd like to leave two and give them to Masako and Ako if that's okay? I know they'll love it."

Kinoshita went ahead and added two more pieces.

Otoha returned to the collections sorting room and gave Masako and Ako two pieces each of the chocolate caramel, telling them what Mr. Kinoshita had said about them.

"It's really sweet and good," Masako said.

"For sure," agreed Ako.

The two of them enjoyed eating the dessert and Ako brewed fresh cups of hot green tea for all of them.

"I actually made these myself once," she said. "Chocolate caramels. Twice."

"You did?" Otoha said.

"The first time was years ago. It was probably the same recipe Mr. Kinoshita used. Since I made it from the book *Anne of Green Gables' Cooking Notes*. I think the book's over forty years old."

"It was written that long ago?"

"First, you make taffy. Which isn't easy. You have to gather all the ingredients . . . condensed milk, butter, sugar, thick malt syrup."

"Mr. Kinoshita said that, too, that it's hard to make."

"You measure them all out and simmer in a pot for about an hour. Until it turns brown. You remember the scene in *Anne of Green Gables* where Anne and Diana try it and burn it? That's what I'm talking about."

"Right."

"The kitchen got all sticky with condensed milk and syrup. But the end product was so delicious. Melt chocolate into that and you get chocolate caramel."

"So that's how you make it!" Otoha exclaimed.

"The second time I made it was just before I came here. Raw caramel was popular for a time, remember?"

"I do. The kind made by a farm in Hokkaido."

"Right. And a thought hit me then, that that raw

caramel was the same as taffy. And I made some at home again. Using the same recipe from the same book."

"That must have been hard."

"You'd think so, but it wasn't. In the past you had to measure out all these sticky things like syrup and condensed milk one by one and then pour them into the pot . . . but now there are digital scales. You can measure them correctly just by putting the pot on the scale and adding the ingredients directly to it. And the pot's now made of Teflon. I was surprised how quickly I could make it without messing up the kitchen."

"But Mr. Kinoshita kept saying how hard it was to make," Otoha said.

"Well, stirring it is definitely a chore, but compared to the past it's not that hard."

"I can see that."

"But somehow . . . it turned out different from when I made it before."

"Different? How?" Otoha asked.

"It was so delicious in the past, and I was looking forward to it so much, so I made it very carefully, poured it into the baking dish, and let it cool slowly . . . I cut it into squares with a heated knife and it was finally ready. And then I tossed a piece into my mouth."

"And . . .?"

"It didn't taste that good."

"Wh—?"

"It was okay, but not as good as in the past. It wasn't that outside-of-this-world taste I remember. So delicious you'd want to fight over the last piece." Ako said this last bit in a low voice, almost a whisper.

"Maybe that was because it was a different age," Masako said. "Nowadays we have so many delicious things to eat."

Does that explain it? Otoha wondered, not at all sure.

She felt like Ako had just expressed something important.

But as she was about to open her mouth to speak, her eyes met Masako's, and Masako shook her head slightly. Otoha kept her mouth shut.

"Yeah, that must be it," Masako said, smiling.

"Make it for us next time," she went on. "Chocolate caramel. Taffy would be fine, too. When we're in Minami's room watching the drama version of *Anne of Green Gables*. If you feel like it, Ako, and it's not too much trouble, of course."

"That's an idea," Ako said, smiling faintly.

Somehow Otoha had the feeling they wouldn't be eating Ako's caramel.

THE COPY OF *SCHOOLGIRL* without the stamp was left in the Lost and Found box. Those manning the reception desk took turns reading it whenever there weren't any users coming in.

"This book's really good." Minami in particular liked it and often reread it. "I might've read it once back in high school, but it didn't leave much of an impression. I'd forgotten about it until now."

"Really?" Otoha said.

"I think back then I couldn't get it and took it as a just a story about some miserable girl, so I didn't like it. Now when I read it, though, it really sinks in."

"Right, right," Otoha said, nodding.

"There are so many parts in it where I feel like I can understand their feelings. I used to be embarrassed to read those, like my own emotions were being laid bare for all to see. But now it strangely moves me."

"Which of Dazai's works did you like best, Minami?"

"I guess his retelling of fairy tales, *Otogibanashi*."

"Yeah, I can see that. 'Cause you're so cheerful and lively."

"But I'm not!"

Minami's voice was so loud it startled Otoha.

"Oh, I'm sorry," she said.

"No, no, I apologize. I've never been called that before and it surprised me."

Minami quickly apologized, yet Otoha was left feeling uncomfortable for a time.

It was a few weeks after this that the strange request came in to the Night Library.

> I have something I'd like to talk over with you all, so tomorrow I'm holding a meeting. Please come at four to the first-floor conference room.

This email went out from Sasai to all the library staff.

When Otoha arrived at the meeting room at four, Sasai and Tokai were already seated at the conference tables and chairs arranged in a circle. She placed her bag on the seat nearest the entrance, and Tokuda, Masako, Ako, and Minami filed in, one after the other. There was no set seating order, but they naturally arranged themselves according to age and seniority, with the more senior people seated farthest from the door.

The first-floor conference room was a simple setup, just tables and chairs. On occasion it was used as a larger reception room when they had a lot of guests, but right now it temporarily housed Tadasuke Shirakawa's books, stacked in cardboard boxes in one corner. It had been two months since the incident with Tamura when they'd been brought here from the warehouse, and there hadn't been an opportunity to return them, so here they sat.

"We don't often have this kind of meeting, but today I wanted to hear everyone's opinion."

EPISODE THREE

Sasai waited to speak until everyone was seated.

"I called it a *meeting*, but I'd just like to hear everyone open up and give their honest opinions here."

"Putting it that way actually makes us even more tense, you know," Tokai laughed, and the others nodded in agreement.

"If so, I'm sorry."

Sasai might be apologizing, yet his expression remained fixed.

"But really, I do want to hear everyone's ideas, and keep it informal. There's something that's come up that I can't decide on my own."

Sasai always calmly took care of things at the library, so Otoha felt even more uneasy.

What could it be, something he couldn't *decide* about on his own?

"So, what is it?" Tokuda said, sounding a bit irritated.

"I'm sorry," Sasai said. "Let me start by laying out the facts. The thing is, we've been discussing having Mizuki Takashiro's collection donated here, the books that she collected during her lifetime."

"Huh?"

"*The* Mizuki Takashiro?!"

"For real? Mizuki Takashiro?"

Everyone spoke at once. The most intense reaction, though, was from the younger staff members, with Masako and Ako simply saying, quietly, "Oh really?"

Otoha wanted to say something, but her voice choked up and nothing came out.

"Now, this is really amazing. The biggest author we've had, wouldn't you say, since Ryoichi Kaito?" Tokai was clearly excited. "I genuinely would like to see her collection myself."

"Goodness, isn't *the biggest since Kaito* a bit of an exaggeration?" Masako asked. "Ms. Takashiro was still young and I think comparing her to someone who was nominated for the Nobel is a bit much . . ."

"But in terms of popularity she might even be higher," Tokai said. "Younger people love her books. And she's not just popular, but a formidable talent. She was nominated for both the Akutagawa and Naoki prizes and won prizes abroad too. I was sure she would be the next Japanese writer to win the Nobel. In terms of style, too, she covers so many genres, from science fiction to mystery to horror, as well as serious fiction, and is great in all of them."

"True," Masako agreed.

As the others excitedly discussed things, Otoha found she couldn't get a word out. Tears welled up and rolled down her cheeks. And then she finally found her voice.

"Hold on just a minute . . ." she said.

Everyone looked over at Otoha for the first time. And, noticing the tears, they stared at her in surprise.

"Are you crying? Otoha—what's the matter?" Ako asked. "Were you, maybe, that fond of her? Of Mizuki Takashiro?"

Otoha still couldn't get any words out well, and fluttered her hand in denial.

"No, no, that's not it," she finally sputtered. "It's just that . . ."

She wiped away the tears spilling out.

"This means Mizuki Takashiro is *really dead*," she said.

"What? You didn't know?! It was in the news about three months ago," Minami, beside her, said, handing her a handkerchief. Otoha accepted it and wiped her eyes.

"I knew that," Otoha said. "Of course I did. But I didn't believe it. I mean, I didn't think it was actually true."

Otoha was sniffling loudly and Ako, on her other side, handed her a tissue. Otoha, oblivious of those around her, blew her nose loudly.

"I was sure it was her . . . well, we all called her by a nickname, Takapon. Is it okay to use that name? We thought that was definitely a Takapon kind of joke. We were sure it was some sort of rebirth, maybe, before her next work came out? We were sure there was a deeper reason behind it."

"You mean she spread a rumor that she had died as publicity for her writing?" Masako asked. "Would even Mizuki Takashiro do something like that? It seems unlikely, since there were obituaries in major newspapers and everything." Her opinion certainly had merit.

Mizuki Takashiro was essentially an anonymous writer.

His or her age and gender were never made public, no photograph had ever been seen, and of course the author had never appeared in public, or at awards ceremonies or parties. Other than the novels there were no essays, interviews, or social media presence whatsoever. He/she had only published with one publisher, and the editor in charge had always been the same person, apparently. From the writing style, most people decided the author had to be male, in his thirties, but many of the works were written from a woman's point of view, and there was a news report of a noted middle-aged woman writer who strongly insisted that "Mizuki Takashiro must be a woman. There are several parts in the works that only a woman could have written."

"I mean, no one said that they attended the funeral," Otoha said, "and no one has ever met someone who said they did. The cause of death was never made public, and no one even knows the name of their editor. I can see regular people believing it easily, but I was an employee of a bookstore, yet isn't it strange that not a single rumor reached me?"

The others were all looking at Otoha, a bit dismayed. She knew she should tamp down her emotions here, but the words just spilled out and she couldn't help herself.

"They might be an anonymous writer who doesn't give away any personal information, but they were very kind to their readers. You can tell this if you read their works. I don't think they would just pass away like this . . ." Otoha finally got to the end of her little speech.

"I still can't believe . . . that they're really dead," she added.

"My apologies," Sasai said, bowing to her.

"No, I should be apologizing for having gone off the rails."

"I had no idea you were such a great fan, Ms. Higuchi . . ." Tokai said, a wry smile mixed in, his voice kind.

"I'm not such a huge fan, really, but their avid readers even celebrate their 'birthday' on the day that their debut work came out!" Otoha said.

"I understand," Sasai said solemnly, and this tone of voice made the others burst out laughing. Otoha, too, laughed through her tears.

"Thanks to you, Otoha, I understand Mizuki Takashiro's popularity better now," Masako said. "She really was an amazing writer."

"And we had no idea," Ako added.

"And speaking of which, this is exactly what I wanted

to ask all of you about," Sasai said. "Clearly we'd be happy to receive Takashiro's collection, but I wonder if it's okay to make this public only a few months after their passing."

"If we get the collection and organize it . . . I think it'll take at least half a year after she passed away. We're quite backed up right now," Masako said.

"Of course. Even so, isn't it a bit soon? As we saw from Otoha's reaction, they were tremendously popular. And they left behind a number of riddles and mysteries after they passed away. If we make their collection public there will be throngs of people coming here . . . which may be hard to handle. And we'd have to be on the lookout for thefts as well."

"I see. So that's been worrying you," Tokai said, nodding. "I think we can avoid that to some extent. We set up a special room for the collection, tightly control people coming in and out, don't let people bring in anything of their own, and so on. And of course have someone stationed there to keep watch."

"Yes, we could, and to some extent we can prevent any theft," said Sasai. "But more than that is the question of whether we really should make the collection public. A collection is extremely personal information."

"Oh," Otoha said despite herself. "Because all kinds of things would come out?"

"Right. The gender of the author, for instance, age—information that Takashiro never made public will possibly get leaked. It only stands to reason, but also which books the author liked. Things that until now were kept under wraps."

"But the family is saying it's okay to make it public, aren't they? Or was this Takashiro's dying wish?" Tokai asked.

"The one we spoke with was their younger sister. And truthfully that was all a bit delicate . . . " Sasai said.

"Delicate?" An unusual word for Sasai, Otoha thought. A rather vague term for him.

"I'm the one who took the call," Sasai said. "Just from talking with her over the phone it was clear she was worked up about it . . . At any rate, she said, 'I want to get rid of the books.' Said they're an eyesore."

"An eyesore!" Otoha had merely repeated Sasai's word, yet her unspoken message—one they all seemed to pick up on—was *Eyesore? What a rude thing to say! She might be Takapon's sister, but that is unacceptable!*

"No, actually the first one to get in touch was a publisher that Takashiro worked with. Told me that Takashiro had died suddenly and their family wanted to dispose of their things. Said that at this rate, they were going to have a company come and sell off everything today or tomorrow. The person from the publisher didn't know what to do, but felt it was a shame for the collection to be broken up and scattered like that. And he asked if we could accept the collection at our library, at least for now."

"So that's what happened?"

"The person from the publishers also seemed a little upset. He didn't have any other place to put the books, though. He said they'd never had a case like this before and were at their wits' end."

Otoha recalled that Mizuki Takashiro's publisher was a relatively small one, with the same editor, which made it easier to keep things secret.

"I also talked with her," Sasai went on. "This is an unusual way of handling it, but the younger sister said she wanted us to come to the house to get the collection. She said she would give the collection to us if we would pack up the books and take them away. And also . . ." He hesitated here. ". . . I don't know if I should mention this, but . . . how should I put it? . . . That sister seemed quite . . . eccentric."

Deciding that after just one phone call, she must be really something, Otoha thought.

"I got the feeling that if she said she'd get rid of them in a few days, she really meant it."

"So what's puzzling you, Mr. Sasai?" Tokuda, quiet up till now, asked.

"Not sure if puzzled is right. I wanted to hear everyone's opinion on this. The impact on us might be more than we'd like. I'm not sure where they heard it from, but members of the media have already gotten in touch with me, asking to see the collection as soon as it's open to the public. Even a freelance writer asking to see it before it's open to the public. They seem really interested in seeing it, figuring it'll provide clues to the authors' gender and age and interests."

"They should contact the younger sister about that directly. Has there been no coverage?" Tokuda asked, looking perplexed.

"The publisher is stopping it." Sasai smiled. "The publisher convinced the sister that it's better to keep Mizuki Takashiro a mystery, that that would help with future sales of their books, and will help the sister avoid contact with the media. They apparently convinced her. At the same time, the sister said she wants to dispose of the house and assets, and they can't stop her doing that, of course. She wants to get rid of the belongings and sell the house."

"Sounds kind of messed up," Tokai laughed. "When I worked in a used bookstore there would sometimes be those kind of places that disposed of collections, so I kind of get it."

"That's right, you were in the used book trade, weren't you?" Masako murmured.

"Yes," Tokai said. "It happens a lot, actually. The family doesn't realize the value of books and sells them all off. Not just individual books, but whole collections as well."

Tokai turned to Sasai. "Three months—usually during that time the family would finish with the forty-ninth day memorial for the deceased, and then start discussing what to do about gravesites and the inheritance. And if the deceased had any debts or loans, that would be the time they look into whether these can be waived, and it would only be after that that they think about any property or things left behind by the deceased."

"Right."

"Does Mizuki Takashiro have any other heirs, other than the younger sister?" Tokai asked.

"None, as far as I heard," Sasai said.

"That's something you better look into carefully, otherwise there could be problems down the road," Tokai said. "If other family members pop up and demand that the books be returned, there could be trouble. And by then the books will all be stamped with the collection stamp."

"Right. And since the author is gone, we'll have to talk with the sister about the design for the stamp." A point that Masako, the person in charge of sorting collections, noticed.

"I don't know . . . it all sounds like a terrible amount of trouble!" Minami said, head in hands, pressing her temples.

"But let's accept them! That much we absolutely *must do*!" Otoha couldn't help voicing this loudly. No matter what, she wanted to defend that point. It was a shock to know for certain that the author had died, but if it were true, they were the best people to handle the collection, she figured.

"I've only been working in this library for two months," she went on, "but we have the know-how to handle collections, and above all everyone here loves writers and books! And as a fan of Takashiro I want you all handling it. Because I trust you!"

Masako and Ako, and all the others looked at each other and smiled. The atmosphere quickly softened.

"Thank you very much for the compliment," Masako said.

"Yes, of course I have no objection either. It'll be troublesome, but Takashiro's books will be a real asset for us." Minami's words now, not opposing it, were at odds with her earlier gesture.

"Did the—owner say anything about it?" Masako asked.

A small, but certain tension ran through the group.

"The owner is basically in agreement," Sasai said, "but said it will be quite time-consuming and wanted to hear everyone's opinions. Which is why I called this meeting. After this I will report on what was said here." Sasai glanced around at the group with a serious look. "I take it the consensus is that we should accept the books?"

They all nodded, some like Otoha more enthusiastically, others like Tokuda, more grudgingly.

"We could have problems like with Mr. Shirakawa, and we've seldom retrieved a collection directly from a home. And since we don't know how many volumes we're talking about it's hard to say anything definite . . . though the sister did say there were *lots* of books."

"That doesn't tell us much. *Lots* means something quite different for those who are regular readers and those who aren't." At Ako's words the group all nodded deeply.

"And let's discuss whether the collection should be made public, and if so when and how. I imagine we'll want to consult with the publisher as well," Sasai said.

"When are we going to go get the books?" Ako asked.

"The sooner the better. The sister could very well change her mind," Sasai said. "If possible, today, or at the latest tomorrow or the day after. I'll call her again, but since it's late already, I would think sometime tomorrow, during the day."

Sasai looked over at Tokai.

"I definitely would like you to come, Mr. Tokai. You're the most used to this type of situation."

"Of course. No problem," Tokai said.

"Let me go with you too!" Otoha called out, seizing the moment. It was truly sad that Takapon was dead, but if it was true and she didn't go, she knew she'd deeply regret it.

"Really . . . ?" Sasai said, evasively. "I was thinking it best if men go, since it will be hard work. And we don't know how many books we're talking about."

That sounded like a fib. Hadn't Sasai asked her to go along when they retrieved Shirakawa's collection?

Tokai spoke softly. "It is indeed a tough job. With things left behind by the recently deceased, the spirit of the person is still lingering there, more than you might expect. And with a fan . . . and one that broke down in tears like that, well, there's a chance you'll cause a scene again, sobbing. We don't know what sort of stance the family has and certainly don't want to do anything to rile them up."

"I won't!" Otoha insisted. "I won't cause a scene, I promise. Don't you think it's better to have a woman along with you?! I don't know the situation at Takapon's home now, but if the sister is alone, she might find it frightening to have a bunch of men barge in. And there might be places where only a woman would be able to enter."

Otoha desperately tried to make her case.

"You do have a point." Sasai nodded. "Okay, but

promise me you absolutely won't cry. If you do cry, I'll send you out of the room and you'll be in charge of carrying boxes from the door to the car."

"I understand," Otoha said.

"And could you come as well, Mr. Tokuda? I need a man to help carry the boxes."

Sasai looked over at Tokuda.

"That's fine with me." Tokuda nodded, his face blank.

"And I'm thinking of having our library detective, Mr. Kuroiwa, come with us. Since he knows a lot about legal issues. I'll have him on standby in the car if we need him."

"If the weather's good, could we take a small pickup truck too?" Tokai said. "We don't know how many books we're talking about. I'll ask a friend from back when I was in used books to see if we can borrow his."

"Yes, please do so."

AFTER THE MEETING, SASAI contacted the sister and set a time for the following day.

When Otoha went out in front of the library after twelve, the members going were all waiting there . . . Sasai, Tokai, Tokuda, and Kuroiwa. Parked there were the HiAce van they'd used before, and a small truck.

"Alright, let's go," Sasai said.

Tokai looked over at Otoha.

"Ms. Higuchi, today could you ride in the truck with me? Little pickup trucks like this are kind of fun to ride in. And also I had something I'd like to talk with you about before we get to the house."

"Of course."

As Otoha got in and sat down beside Tokai, she wondered what he wanted to say to her.

"I'm looking forward to working with you today," Otoha said.

"Yes. Me too."

Last evening Tokai had said some pretty pointed things to her about her outburst, but today he'd changed completely and was gentle and easygoing.

"Um, what was it you wanted to tell me?" Otoha asked this after they had gotten on the highway.

"I'm sorry about yesterday. I said some pretty harsh things to you." Tokai glanced over at her and grinned.

"That's quite alright. I really made a scene and am kind of embarrassed."

"No, it's perfectly understandable, you being such a big fan and all . . ."

"I understand the author's dead, and I mourned then, so I'm okay now. It's just that yesterday the name came up so suddenly and I didn't expect it at all."

"I know."

"And they never announced the cause of death

either . . . Maybe I couldn't handle it, emotionally, more than I realized."

"Um."

There was silence between them for a moment. *The death of a young person . . . and if that person was also an author—how could I not think about it?* Otoha thought. The thought that maybe Takapon herself chose to die.

"Well, what I wanted to tell you today was a few things you should be careful of after we get to that house," Tokai said, nimbly changing the subject.

"I appreciate that."

"I already told the others this, but I wanted to tell you in particular, Ms. Higuchi."

"Because I was a fan?"

"That's part of it, yes. The chances are that the sister is around the same age as you. Women that age are especially aware of each other."

"I'd say that's true."

"I have no idea how she's going to approach your being there. She might find it easy to talk with you since you're the same age, but the opposite's a possibility too."

"So what should I do?"

"Just act neutral. No matter how she reacts, I'd like you to just casually go about your job."

"I understand."

"And this is something to keep in mind when you

work at someone else's house, but pay attention to your gaze."

"My gaze?"

"That's right. Don't let your eyes wander around, or focus or stare at anything."

"I wouldn't do that!" Otoha couldn't help but laugh.

"I don't think you're that kind of person, but the owner of the home will be very sensitive about that. It sounds like the younger sister wasn't living with the author, and we don't know what the situation is in the house. Sorry to keep repeating this, but since you're a woman of the same generation, be careful not to look around the rooms. You're not used to this kind of work, so it's best to keep your gaze down."

"Keep my gaze down?"

"Exactly."

Otoha let out a sigh.

"I'm sorry. I didn't mean to make you so nervous," Tokai said.

"It's okay."

"I'm wondering, though, what kind of home it is . . . The address is in Kawasaki City, in Kanagawa Prefecture . . ."

There was no car navigation system in the little pickup truck. As Tokai followed the car in front that Sasai was driving, he glanced at the memo with the address.

"It might be near Musashi-Kosugi. I wonder if it's one of those high-rise condos," Otoha said.

"That's possible, based on the address. But if you get away from the station there are still a lot of older houses and smaller apartment buildings."

"I think it would be typical for Takapon to live in either a high-rise condo or an old single house."

"I can see that. Though I've only read the author's debut work."

As they talked, the area filled with high-rise condos grew closer.

"So it's high-rise condos after all," Tokai said as they watched Sasai's car get sucked down into an underground parking lot in one of the towers. The buildings were condos yet had cafes and restaurants on the first floor and parking lots apparently open to nonresidents.

As planned, they asked Kuroiwa to wait behind in the car.

"Takashiro really must have made a bundle," Tokai said lightly, laughing, as they took the elevator after the concierge had shown them the way. The unit was on the top floor.

"Do you think it's true that the upper floors are more expensive?" Tokuda said, blinking his eyes in wonder at it all. He seemed a little tense.

The elevator was apparently shared by two apartments on each floor. Mizuki Takashiro's unit was right in front them when they exited the elevator.

"Well, I guess we'd better do it," Sasai said as he rang the doorbell.

"Coming!" a woman's voice called out. Maybe the younger sister?

The heavy door swung open and a young woman's face emerged. No makeup, her expression vacant.

"Hello, my name's Sasai. We spoke on the phone yesterday."

The concierge had no doubt called up to alert the woman, but Sasai introduced himself again.

"Um. Come in."

That's all she said before she proceeded into the apartment. Sasai hurriedly stopped the door from shutting in their faces. The woman's curt greeting was, Otoha thought, either because she was basically rude and unfriendly, or else because she wasn't used to meeting people like this.

As soon as she was inside, Otoha realized why Takashiro's sister looked so out of it. In one hand, the woman was holding a can of what was obviously an alcoholic drink.

She was happy Tokai had warned her ahead of time.

EPISODE FOUR

SEIKO TANABE'S SIMMERED SARDINES AND OKARA

Inside the apartment of the anonymous writer Mizuki Takashiro there was, first, a long hallway, which led to a spacious living room. One of the walls inside was all glass, so the room was bright and full of sunlight.

A large can of an alcoholic drink in one hand, Takashiro's younger sister looked at them, eyes blinking. Most likely, Otoha thought, until now she'd been holed up in some other dark room, drinking.

You're on the top floor, in such a sunny space, Otoha thought, *so what a complete waste.*

"May we go ahead, then, and start boxing up the books?" Sasai asked, and the woman merely nodded.

They didn't need to ask where the collection was, for

one wall of the living room was floor-to-ceiling bookshelves crammed full of books. A lovely space. *I'm envious of anyone able to live here*, Otoha thought. How nice it would be to read with the sunlight streaming in, and late at night, too, with the night view laid out before you.

"Are there other bookshelves too?"

"There are. There are books in the study, in the bedroom . . . even in the lavatory."

When Sasai looked surprised she smiled a little.

"That's why I told you there are a *lot*."

"I understand. We brought along as many cardboard boxes as we could, so I think we'll be okay, though please allow us some time to do it."

"As you wish."

The woman plunked herself down on the sofa in the living room. The sofa was large and low, surrounding an equally low table. A quite comfortable spot. As soon as she sat down, though, she flopped down heavily onto her back.

"Let me know when you're finished," she said.

Tokai's advice to keep her eyes to herself, to not look around the room, helped out at first, Otoha thought, but now it was a bit pointless, perhaps, for Takashiro's younger sister's own eyes were shut.

"I'll go pack up the books in the bathroom," Otoha told Sasai and the others in a soft voice and they nodded.

EPISODE FOUR

She carried a cardboard box and went in search of the toilet. *Probably it's the first door after we entered*, she thought, and sure enough it was.

Otoha asked to pack up the bathroom since she figured the books there would be ones only a fan like herself could be able to take care of. And for one other reason . . .

"Whoa." She tried to stifle her surprise but couldn't.

Takashiro's toilet room was about three tatami mats in size. And there, too, were shallow bookshelves reaching to the ceiling, mostly filled with manga and paperbacks.

Since the room was fairly spacious, it wasn't as untidy as she'd expected. Had Takashiro read these books while in the bathroom, or did they put the shelves in there to handle the overflow the other rooms couldn't? It was probably a little of both.

Up high in the room was a storage shelf with a door, the kind you find in most houses. A place to store toilet paper and so on.

Otoha was curious about it, but made sure not to touch it.

The manga were almost all famous ones—complete sets of *One Piece, Jojo's Bizarre Adventure, Demon Slayer: Kimetsu no Yaiba, Glass Mask, Chibi Maruko Chan*. Nothing there to indicate the author's gender or age.

The small cardboard box she brought was soon full, so she went to get some more.

In the living room, Sasai and Tokai were taking books down from the shelves.

"So what're you going to do with those books?" the younger sister, sacked out on the sofa, asked them.

"We'll take them back to the library, organize them, and then make them available for the public to view," Otoha said.

"I know that. I mean what's the first thing you do with them when you get back?"

"First we stamp each book with a collection stamp and make a record of what kind of books they are."

"Hmm."

She didn't seem to have any particular aim in asking.

Otoha returned to the toilet and continued boxing up books.

When she was nearly done, she couldn't restrain herself and opened up the high shelf.

All she found were spare rolls of toilet paper and tissue boxes. No makeup or women's products or anything of that nature.

She felt suddenly deflated. So it seemed Mizuki Takashiro was a man, after all.

She resumed packing when the door to the toilet opened.

EPISODE FOUR

"My gosh!" Taken by surprise she looked up to see Takashiro's sister standing there.

"Aren't you overreacting?"

"I'm sorry! Do you need to use the room?" Otoha asked.

"Uh-uh. I just wanted to see what you were doing. I got tired of watching the others."

"Can I continue, then?"

"Sure."

As Otoha went on packing away books the sister stood behind her, leaning against the wall.

"Is it because you're a woman?" she asked.

"Excuse me?"

The sudden question took Otoha by surprise.

"Is it because you're a woman that you volunteered for bathroom duty?"

"No, that isn't it."

"Isn't it because of the persistent idea that cleaning toilets is women's work? Unconsciously, aren't you thinking that?"

"No . . ."

I took this on because I'm a fan, Otoha wanted to say, and more than that out of curiosity . . . but she couldn't say this, and the more she was asked about it the less sure she felt. Maybe she did have feelings like that . . .

"You know that when they catch terrorists who've

committed mass murder, they're forced to clean toilets, and some people have raised a huge ruckus, calling it humiliation and abuse."

"Huh?"

"You didn't know that?"

"No, I didn't," Otoha said.

"In their countries, for religious reasons they don't let men clean toilets. They see it as work fit only for slaves or women. They well may be terrorist criminals, but making prisoners do that is abuse, some insist."

"Really?"

"It's awful. We women are being asked to do work that's even below terrorist criminals."

She fairly spit this out, then turned on her heels and left.

Otoha felt strangely uneasy.

The feeling like . . . she'd forgotten something very important.

ONCE SHE'D PACKED UP all the books in the bathroom, she returned to the living room.

Sasai and Tokai were there, moving about briskly, still boxing up the collection from the wall shelves.

"Shall I help out?" she asked them.

"No, but could you pack up what's in the other

rooms? Tokuda is boxing up books in the study, but probably elsewhere . . ." Sasai said, when Otoha, noticing him looking behind her, turned around and found the younger sister there.

"There are books in other rooms too," the sister said. She nodded reluctantly.

"So we should check each of the other rooms? If that's alright with you . . . Ms. . . . Takashiro?"

He knew Takashiro was a pen name but had no other way of addressing her.

The younger sister, predictably, raised an eyebrow.

"I'm not Takashiro."

"I'm sorry, I didn't know what to call you."

"You can call me . . . Mone."

Mone Takashiro, Otoha repeated to herself, spontaneously engraving the name in her mind.

"Ms. Mone? Which kanji do you write that with?"

"Is that necessary right now? It's not my real name."

"Pardon me."

"Then it's okay to go around the rooms? Are there places you'd rather we don't go in?" Otoha cut in, finding it hard to see Sasai keep on apologizing.

"You've already seen the lavatory, so why not? I don't care," the woman said.

Otoha put together a few cardboard boxes and carried them with her as she made the rounds of the other rooms.

First she went back toward the bathroom—the lavatory in the sister's words—and opened the door next to it. Behind it was a bathroom with a glass partition, in front of which was a washbasin, and opposite that a large washer and dryer and a shelf.

Otoha was sure there wouldn't be any books here, but as she began to shut the door she heard Mone's voice.

"Over this way."

Mone opened the shelf below the vanity where, next to extra toothbrushes, toothpaste, and shampoo there was a tight stack of books. She looked more closely and saw it was a set of the complete works of Atsuko Suga. Not paperbacks, but hardbound, boxed volumes. All nine volumes packed tightly together, vertically and horizontally.

"I see, Astuko Suga," Otoha let out.

"You know her?"

"Atsuko Suga?"

The sister nodded.

"Yes, I like her a lot," Otoha said.

"Hmm." She nodded again, seemingly not very interested.

"Is it really alright for us to take these?"

"What?"

"I mean . . . these are really nice books."

"What're you talking about? I had you come here to take *all* the books away."

"Yes, you're right, of course."

EPISODE FOUR

Otoha was reaching out for them when the sister said, "And the ones here."

The cabinet above the washing machine had doors on it. When she opened them inside were two face towels and two bath towels and next to them, more books.

These were a set of the complete works of Seiko Tanabe. Ten volumes, again tightly packed together both vertically and horizontally.

"There should be other volumes as well," Otoha said.

"How come?"

"I don't think this is a complete set."

"I don't know. Maybe they're in another room?"

"Is that right?"

The little cardboard box was soon almost full, and awfully heavy.

Wow, this is going to be one backbreaking job, Otoha thought. *We don't just have to pack up the books, but carry them all downstairs . . . how long is this all going to take, anyway?*

Trying to not think too much about what was next, Otoha opened the door to the room across the hall from the bathroom. This was the study, where Tokuda, too, was struggling mightily.

"Are you okay, Mr. Tokuda?" she asked.

"Um." Facing the bookshelves, he didn't look over at her.

"If there's anything I can do to help, please let me know."

"Ah." Now he finally turned in her direction. "If you go to the living room, bring me back a few more cardboard boxes."

"I'm on it."

Next to the study was an eight-mat–sized bedroom with a built-in closet.

There was a double bed with white sheets and a dark brown comforter. This took up so much of the room, there was little else there.

Other than the double bed there was little distinctive about the space. No aroma candles, no paintings of flowers. Probably when you turned off the lights, drew the thick curtains, and shut the door it was pitch-black. But for that reason alone it must make it easy to relax there. When Takashiro took a break from writing, he/she must have lain here to take a rest.

A double bed, huh? No, a double bed would be easy to sleep in. Even people by themselves sometimes chose that instead of a single.

"There are books in the closet."

Once again the younger sister, Mone, spoke out and it startled her.

"Well then," Otoha said, ready to begin, but Mone said, "Hold on a second."

She stood in front of Otoha, waving her off, as if telling her to step away. And Otoha stepped back a few feet.

"It's okay to look inside. Go ahead."

The closet was open wide. It was a simple design, with hanging rods for hangers and nothing else. There were clothes in only about half the space, almost all white shirts and black trousers. The other half were bookshelves packed in tightly, almost up to the rods and nearly as deep as the closet itself. They seemed to have been made to fit, and Otoha wondered if they were custom made.

"Amazing. Even in here," she couldn't help saying.

"What is?" Mone asked.

"Other possessions have been kept to a minimum, so there'd be room for books."

"I wonder. Takashiro didn't have many things to begin with. Other than books. I don't think Takashiro needed to minimize other belongings."

This was the first time she'd said anything about Mizuki Takashiro as a person. Otoha turned around. Mone seemed to have noticed the same thing, and looked away.

Otoha said no more and packed away books in the boxes. She wanted to hear more about Takashiro, but if she said too much, she was afraid Mone would change her mind and clam up.

The shelves here were deep, and many of them contained larger volumes, collections of photographs and artwork detailing all sorts of people and scenes. Only two of the photo collections were ones of women, of the popular idol singers Hiroko Yakushimaru and Tomoyo

Harada, both when they were in their teens. Neither of which provided any more concrete clues about Takashiro.

As Otoha was packing these away Mone opened up the closet next to it. Otoha glanced over and saw a dresser inside about as tall as her. Above that were more shelves.

The shelves were, of course, packed with books, and Mone was opening the dresser drawers one by one to check if there were books inside.

Thank you, Otoha was about to say, but stifled the words.

There was probably underwear in the drawers. Seeing those would provide more clues about Takashiro, so Mone was going through them herself.

Despite all her apparent indifference, maybe Mone cared after all.

ORGANIZING BOOKS LIKE THIS in someone's home really brings back memories.

I was a used book dealer for over ten years, Tokai thought, and I still *am*. I've never considered myself a library staff member, even once.

I've never told others in the used book trade, or people here, but the first place I worked was one of those new-style big box bookstores, a new/used bookstore, you might call it.

When I was in high school, I started working there along the highway back in my hometown. The type of store that doesn't just sell books, but also CDs, videos, and game software. The kind of shop you find in any town.

In that sort of place, you don't need any special knowledge or skill when it comes to purchasing books. They were simply judged by how new, clean, and popular they were, though they didn't like ones that sold too well, ones we had too many copies of. With old books, we'd just clean them up, using sandpaper to clean off what was called in the trade the *upper* part, the outside of the pages, which get faded and dirty, and then sell them. I had no knowledge of rare or specialized books, and even now it makes me shudder to think about how I used to sandpaper the covers of such high-class volumes like those published by Shincho Bunko and Iwanami Bunko. Books that would have brought a high price at the Kanda used bookstore district in Tokyo were sometimes treated as *worthless*, and though valuable, we'd refuse to purchase them, and even threw them out at times. I occasionally wondered if maybe those might be valuable.

"It's just *noise*," the mid-thirties store manager at the time said.

This was when I showed him a volume, a signed copy of the debut work by a popular novelist, saying, "This should bring a high price, shouldn't it?"

"Nah, don't need it. Toss it."

"Are you sure?"

The manager wanted to get rid of it because it was missing its slipcover. That's when he made the comment about it being *just noise*.

"Huh?" I said.

"This kind of book is old but it does have value. If not noise, then, call it a *bug*."

"A bug?"

What did it mean that an old book was like a bug? Like a glitch that scrambled a computer's programming?

"Something like this throws the system out of whack. Makes it hard to decide things. I want to judge books only on their age and condition. Whatever obstructs that, I . . ."

He shook his head, as if unable to think of the right words.

What he may have wanted to say was "I don't like them" or "I won't allow them." But that would have been a bit over-the-top, so he left it unspoken.

The manager was married and had two children. Though far from the train station, he lived near the main road in a brand-new three-bedroom house he'd purchased when he got married, in what was considered the prime residential neighborhood in that area, and also drove a brand-new minivan. He'd taken out loans for both the house and the car. He'd bring his kids to the store sometime to play, and his pretty, young wife carried a designer bag, one he'd surely taken out a loan for as well. People in my hometown built a new home when they got married. Compared to Tokyo, land was dirt cheap, but a large house cost as much as 200–300K. If you didn't have one, you weren't considered a full-fledged adult. Naturally there were a lot of used houses for sale when couples got divorced. But people ignored these in favor of building new ones. This was so unusual that a few years before, a nationwide TV variety show, thinking these customs and local color were curious, featured it in a special program, though locals scratched their heads, wondering what was so strange about it.

City people would probably laugh at this store manager, who tossed rare books into the trash, and call him a barbarian. But that wasn't right. He had the words to discuss his mindset, which he explained to me, a high school student at the time. There were many people in that town, and in fact in Tokyo too, who couldn't articulate things as well as he did.

But calling these books "bugs" or "noise that threw things out of whack" meant the manager had, inside him, a guilty conscience for doing so.

"I don't like this. That type," the manager said, still muttering to himself.

"Why do books have to be this complicated?" he

went on. "I don't get it. Are there refrigerators that are more valuable just because they're old? I wouldn't mind if there were, but our store doesn't deal in those."

"I understand."

"The author's signature is just like a stain."

Don't get me wrong, I didn't dislike the guy. All I had to do was come to work right on time, and greet the manager, then I never got into trouble about my hairstyle or the clothes I wore. And if a book was damaged, he'd let me take it home without himself checking it. That's exactly why I chose to work there.

When we told customers they couldn't purchase a used book from them and asked if they wanted us to dispose of it, almost a hundred percent of them left the books there and went home. An older boy from my high school who worked there told me that books and manga with dirty covers or pages, or ones missing covers, or ones that sold so well their storage area was overflowing with them, I could take these home whenever I wanted.

I loved to read books and manga. But I wasn't so well off I could buy that many, and it was too much trouble to use the school library.

Cardboard boxes and paper bags overflowing with books that were to be discarded sat piled in a corner of the yard behind the store. While I was working, I'd check those for any books I was after, and when

EPISODE FOUR

work was done I'd carefully choose some and take them home with me. I was young and didn't care about their condition. If you could read them, that worked for me.

And I also stealthily took home ones the manager labelled *noise* . . . ones signed by the author, first editions, old-looking paperbacks. It didn't mean all that much to me. It felt the same as when kids collect pretty stones or acorns. I just found it hard to throw away things that possibly had some value.

When I was a junior in high school, some friends and I took a four-day, three-night trip to Tokyo. It took two and a half hours by the Hokuriku Shinkansen train. One friend who was into clothes said he wanted to go to Harajuku, while another, an otaku type, wanted to check out Akihabara. And all of us agreed we had to visit Shibuya. So we decided that the morning of our last day we'd each go off on our own and do our thing.

I suddenly decided I'd take some of the used books I'd collected and sell them at a used bookstore in Tokyo. All my other friends had their own interests and places they wanted to go. Truthfully, though, there wasn't anywhere I was dying to visit, so I decided to stop by Kanda, the big used bookstore district.

For four days I lugged around ten heavy volumes with me. On our last day in Tokyo I got off at Jinbocho Station. I had no idea which store to go into, so I chose the biggest one I saw on the main street. Inside near the entrance there were piles of collected works sets and specialized books. I was young and reckless back then. If it were me now, I'd never be brave enough to go in.

The old owner seated in the rear of the store looked over my books. "A hundred yen," he said.

"Huh?" I couldn't help saying.

"I'll give you a hundred yen for them."

"For *all* of them?"

He nodded.

"So are you going to leave them, or take them back?"

"Um, I'll leave them," I said.

That might be cheap, but I wasn't about to keep lugging them around Tokyo. For the first time I understood the feeling of the customers in our store back home when they were told their books were worthless, but still left them with us.

So these *are* pretty cheap, I thought. Our manager was right after all.

The owner turned around, took some money out of a drawer behind him and placed a hundred-yen coin in my hand.

"Thank you."

Disappointed, I was on my way out of the shop, head drooping, when an idea came to me. I should check out what's selling for a high price here. What kind of books does a place like this have for sale?

"Young man!"

As I looked around the books, the owner called out to me.

"Yes?"

"Come here for a second, son."

"Okay."

I returned to the register.

"So, young fellow. Are you interested in doing this?"

"*This?*"

"Selling books like this . . ."

"No, that's not why I . . ."

Without being prompted, I told him how I'd acquired the books and about the store I worked at back in my hometown.

"Hmm. I sort of thought that might be the case."

"I'm sorry to waste your time with discarded books," I said.

"Well now, about these books you brought . . ."

The owner pointed to one paperback among the pile I'd brought. It was still next to the register and lacked a cover.

"This one's worth a hundred yen, but the others are basically worthless."

"I see . . ."

"About this writer's autograph," he said, pointing to the signed copy of the debut work by a popular author. The book I was sure was worth the most.

"This one's no good since there are too many in circulation. 'Cause the book sold really well. But this paperback is out of print and the author's popular among dilettantes. I'd give you more if it had a cover. But a hundred yen for one without a cover isn't a bad price."

"Is that right?"

"You actually have a good eye for books."

"Really?!"

"However down on your luck you might be, you sold a book to Ikkyodo in Kanda, one you picked out of the trash in a new-style bookstore out in the sticks. Even if it was a fluke, that's pretty impressive, let me tell you."

"Thank you very much."

Without thinking, I bowed in thanks.

"And for a young person these days, you know how to speak politely."

The owner turned around again and from the drawer pulled out two 1000 yen bills and plunked them down in my hand.

"Here you go."

"Huh?"

"A future tip for you. If you spy something promising again, bring it here. If it's good, I'll buy it."

"No—I can't accept this."

I hurriedly held out the bills to him, but he wouldn't take them back, and just grinned.

"It's okay. The next time you're in Tokyo come to my place first to sell anything. That'll be enough. Why don't you have a nice meal before you go back home? The curry place on the corner is pretty well-known."

"Alright . . . Then, thank you so much."

I made one more circuit of the store and then left. It was hard to tell, from just a cursory look around, what books they had, and which ones would sell for high prices. The owner grinned at me again as he watched me.

After that, every time I had some lengthy time off— winter break, spring break, summer—I went to Tokyo to sell some books. Most were discards from the big box store I worked at. At first I hardly sold any, sometimes not even a single one. I checked out shops other than Ikkyodo. Gradually I could sell more books, not just discards, but ones we displayed in our store. I'd buy what I thought could sell for a high price in Kanda. I think I got more skilled over time. Selling books I got free, and ones I paid for myself, was completely different. For the latter, I was betting my own money, wagering on my knowledge that a book would command a high price.

After I started this, I got even more interested in secondhand books. The owner of Ikkyodo told me buying and selling used books to used bookstores like this went by the term *sedori*, meaning a kind of broker. I got hooked on this form of *gambling*. And I decided to go to college in Tokyo. I wanted to study more about used books. I told my parents, though, that I wanted to go into the Japanese literature department in order to become a Japanese high school teacher back home. Though I could have been accepted into a more competitive university, I chose one located in Kanda. I couldn't get enough of old books and of buying and selling them. Part of the attraction might also have been the different values I found in Tokyo and Kanda, the used bookstore area, how the rabble there celebrated the joys of freedom—I was completely captivated by it.

"Are you going to become a *sedori* broker, Tokai?"

The owner of Ikkyodo asked me this the first time I came to the shop after entering college.

"I'm not sure. Now that I'm here I can't very well procure books from back home."

I was planning, though, to make the rounds of bookshops in the suburbs of Tokyo. Online buying and selling had taken off at this point, and there were lots of other ways of doing it.

"What do you think I should do, Mr. Ikkyodo?"

Over time we'd come to call each other by our names. Ikkyodo was the name of the shop, of course, and in the neighborhood, it was the nickname people called the owner by.

"Being a *sedori* is all well and good," the owner said,

EPISODE FOUR

"but I think it's best if you work at a good used bookstore first and learn the trade."

"You think so?"

"How about working here? Part-time."

I couldn't have asked for more. In fact I'd had a faint hope he'd ask me to.

Mr. Ikkyo had a son, my parents' age, and it was decided already that he would take over the shop. So given that I was his grandchildren's age, I knew he thought it was endearing when I'd come to his shop with books.

Once I even heard the owner mutter, *You have a kind of willpower my son lacks.*

And so I became a dealer in used books. I worked part-time for four years, and after graduating from college began working at another used bookstore Mr. Ikkyo introduced me to, and by the time I was in my mid-twenties I had a shop of my own. It was in the part of Kanda very near Akihabara. A tiny little shop specializing mainly in manga and light novels, carrying first editions. Only a fraction of my holdings were displayed in the shop, with most of the profit coming from online sales. For Kanda it was an unusual lineup of books, and thanks to spillover customers from Akihabara, I was able to make a living. In this profession I was pretty young to be independent, and had opened the shop early in my career.

My reason for getting a job in this Night Library is different from the other people working here. In my case, I approached the owner myself.

Before the Night Library had made the news, I'd heard rumors of an odd person who accepted authors' collections and had created a library to house them.

For used bookstores, this could be a matter of life and death, since getting a collection from a deceased author was a veritable treasure trove. There were rare books included, naturally, but also the possibility of signed books. If it was signed by a famous author, it was doubly valuable, with the inscription to the author whose collection it was in.

But a tiny shop like mine had no connections that would lead to a famous author or his family entrusting their collection to me, and I thought this was better than seeing a collection broken up or scattered. With a few exceptions, the owners of other used bookstores in the Kanda vicinity agreed.

And then one day I heard that Mitsumi Tricolor, a famous author in the light novel genre, had suddenly passed away and had left her collection to this Night Library, and the news left me excited.

Mitsumi Tricolor had often stopped by my shop before her books had really started to take off, and I had made out some receipts to her in her real last name, Miumi (which means three oceans), which she'd used when she was still publishing in small coterie magazines. At a certain point, though, the receipts changed to Tricolor Inc.

We'd known each other for several years, and about the time I learned her contact information, since she was leaving books for us to sell, I ventured to ask her, "Are you, by any chance, Ms. Mitsumi Tricolor?" After a moment's hesitation she nodded slightly. I regretted asking, thinking I'd crossed a line. So you can imagine how happy I was the next time she showed up.

After forming this delicate relationship, one day she finally told me, "After I die, I'd like you, Mr. Tokai, to handle all my books. Nobody else knows their value."

Despite that, after she passed away, suddenly those books came not to my shop but here, to the Night Library.

Not that I'm complaining.

If she'd left me her collection, I could have kicked back for a year. (Just an expression, since with all the hard work involved in cataloguing the books and deciding on prices, I would hardly have been twiddling my thumbs.) But with a collection this extensive, one that on its own could constitute a Library of the History of Light Novels, I came to feel it would be better for it to reside in the Night Library.

At the same time, though, I had the feeling that the

books would lie dormant here, wasted, since very few people would ever see them. I felt like with light novels, a relatively recent genre, it would be better to give them to people who really wanted them, who wanted to read them.

At any rate, after Mitsumi Tricolor's death I searched everywhere for the person of the Night Library. I asked the owners of other used bookshops in Kanda, and finally heard at one of the bookstores that the widow of a novelist who'd donated her late husband's collection to the Night Library knew how to get in touch.

So I contacted the owner and managed to wrangle a Skype interview. I told them why I was interested and tried to sell myself.

I'd like you to let me help organize Mitsumi Tricolor's collection, I said . . . *and if there are any books you don't need, I'd like you to let me have them.*

The owner's reply had a caveat—that I accept the following condition.

"You must work at least three years in our library."

I could live with that. Right now my own shop was being run by a person who worked part-time there. And I hadn't gotten even one book from Mitsumi's collection.

I haven't told anybody here this, but that three-year period will be over in six months.

Sometimes I wonder what I'll do when my time is up.

EPISODE FOUR

But I've found the work here more enjoyable than I expected.

When people talk about jobs dealing in books they often list three types—staff in bookstores, librarians, and people working in used bookstores, but there's a conflict of interest among them and the jobs seldom overlap. Sometimes the people are even antagonistic to each other . . . But since working in this little library, I've found those barriers quickly fading.

We all just have different roles to play, I think.

ON THE WAY BACK, everyone was exhausted.

Before they returned to the cars after the visit to Takashiro's high-rise condo, Sasai said to Tokai, Tokuda, and Otoha: "You all should go rest up. The rest of the staff and I can handle it."

"But you're going back to work, aren't you, Mr. Sasai?" Tokai asked, giving a cheerful smile.

"Well, I have to report back to the owner, among other things."

"Then we shouldn't take time off either."

"I think I'll take you up on the offer to go rest. My back's been bothering me," Tokuda said.

"That's no good. You'd better make sure it's okay," Tokai said, nodding to Tokuda.

"I think I will . . . take a break, see how I feel and then come back to work. I might take a day off. But if I do, I'll let you know, Mr. Sasai."

Otoha, too, felt worn out.

"Well, then, I think I'll do the same, and see how I'm feeling. If I can get some sleep, I'll come back to work," Tokai said.

"Please park the cars in front of the building. I'll have others help me unload the boxes."

"Um . . . even if we leave the HiAce as is, wouldn't it be better to take the boxes out of the truck? I get the sense we should be extra careful with this author's books. I'll lend a hand," Kuroiwa murmured. He'd been silent up till now.

"Alright."

"Are you a fan of Mizuki Takashiro, too, Mr. Kuroiwa?!" Otoha couldn't help but ask.

"No. Honestly I heard the name for the first time yesterday, from Mr. Sasai. I checked it out on the internet and got a sense of how her fans and the publishing industry feel about her."

"That's great."

"Then let's just unload the light truck and put the boxes at the entrance. I'm sorry for all the trouble, but thank you," Sasai said, and they all got into the same vehicles they'd ridden out in.

"How was it? . . . Your first time at a late author's

home?" Tokai asked Otoha, silently seated on the passenger side of the light truck.

"I'm not sure what to say."

For a time, she couldn't get any words out. Twilight was approaching and the truck was filled with the glare of the setting sun.

When Otoha didn't say anything for a while, Tokai spoke, echoing Sasai's tone. "You must be tired. Go ahead and take a nap."

"No, I'm fine."

"You sure?"

"I'm sorry, I was just thinking about some things," Otoha said.

"An author you're a big fan of dies and you go to their house—anyone would feel that way." Tokai seemed to be addressing himself.

"No . . . what I was thinking was . . ." Otoha sighed and went on. "The opposite."

"The opposite?" Tokai asked.

"Somehow I just can't feel like Mizuki Takashiro's really dead."

"Even after going to the house?"

"That's part of it. But that's not all . . ." Otoha cocked her head to one side. "I can't really express it well . . . Sorry."

"That's okay. We'll have to organize Takashiro's books, so you'll have plenty of time to clarify your feelings."

"Yeah."

"The good point of our library is that we have lots of time to think."

"Time to think . . . ?"

"The pay is low, we're treated alright, I guess, and the work can be dull at times. But we have plenty of time to think. Don't you feel that way?"

"I never really thought about it," Otoha said. "But I suppose that's true."

"We're not asked to increase sales or anything, and old books don't run away."

"Right."

"Take some time to think about it . . . And one more good thing about our library is you get to talk with people from other occupations."

"Other occupations?"

"You don't often get to work with people who worked in used bookstores, and regular bookstores, as well as former library staff."

"True enough."

"I like that about our job," Tokai said.

Otoha laughed despite herself. And felt better.

That day, she came to work when the library opened, not at the start of regular working hours.

By then all of Mizuki Takashiro's collection had been carried into the meeting room-cum-reception room. When she went to take a look, she found over half the area filled with both Takashiro's and Shirakawa's collections. The room would be out of commission for a while.

"What a huge amount of books. You did a great job."

Otoha turned and saw Masako standing there.

"It must have been a hard job, too, lugging them all the way here from the entrance," Otoha said.

"I suppose so. But it's nothing compared to packing them all up and getting them out of the house," Masako said.

The two of them started heading together to the collections sorting room.

"I guess we'd better start sorting out Mr. Shirakawa's collection pretty soon," Otoha said.

"I talked with Ako about just organizing them as they are, here, instead of taking them to the sorting room. That would mean bumping them up in line, though."

"That might be a good idea."

"Tell me, how was it? Being at Mizuki Takashiro's house?"

Everyone seems so worried about me, Otoha thought, glancing at Masako. Masako looked a bit concerned, of course, yet her expression contained a hint of curiosity as well.

"I told this to Mr. Tokai, too . . ." Otoha began.

"Mmm."

"It was all kind of strange."

"How so?"

"It felt like Takashiro was still alive. I mean, alive and right nearby."

"People's collections can have that effect." Masako nodded.

"No, it wasn't that . . ." Otoha started to say but swallowed back her words.

She felt like she hadn't yet gotten to the point where she could articulate the nagging, uncomfortable feeling she had, and if she did venture to try, it would only lead to something irreparably falling apart.

As always, when they were finished sorting collections they went to the dining hall.

Minami and Tokai were already there, seated in a corner of the cafe. Tokuda, usually there too at this time, had done what he'd said he would, and taken the day off. The two of them had already begun eating.

The cafe owner, Kinoshita, was in the rear, and when Otoha's eyes met his she nodded. She hoped this signaled the message *I'll have the day's staff dinner.*

"Is Mr. Sasai at the reception desk now?" Otoha asked as she sat down next to the two of them.

EPISODE FOUR

"That's right," Minami replied.

Tonight, again, Sasai wasn't eating here. If he did, it always seemed to be at a time when no one else was here.

"How are you feeling? Aren't you tired?" Tokai asked her kindly.

"I feel better than I expected," Otoha said. "I thought if I was really worn out I'd take time off, but I slept and now feel much better."

"Nice to be young."

As they were talking, Kinoshita brought over a tray for her with that night's set menu.

"Tonight's Seiko Tanabe night, I believe?"

"Right."

Every Friday was Seiko Tanabe night. But unlike other authors whose works were the basis for menu items, there wasn't just one menu item on Fridays but several—*okonomiyaki night, Osaka-style oden night*, et cetera.

What he set down in front of her, this night looked like an ordinary set dinner. Brown seemed to be the dominant color, everything kind of simple and humble looking.

"Today's main dish is cooked sardines," Kinoshita explained, "and the side dish is okara, soybean pulp, cooked using the broth from cooking these sardines. This combination appeared several times in her books. It was probably something she herself enjoyed. Plus there's a side dish of *kenchinjiru*, root vegetable soup. This also appears a few times in her essays and novels. The rice is *yukari* rice, rice mixed with dried pickled plums and red shiso flakes."

"I've been meaning to ask you, Mr. Kinoshita, but were you a fan of Seiko Tanabe's works before you came here? She's the only author where you serve so many different dishes."

"No, truthfully I'd never heard of her before. The owner gave me the book *The Many Flavors of Seiko Tanabe*, which came out while the author was still alive, and I planned to make a few of the dishes listed there. In that book they gave the sources for the recipes, and I went ahead and read those too. She wrote a lot about cooking and I really got into it."

"Is that right?"

"I couldn't just decide on one dish and ended up cooking quite a few."

Otoha sipped some of the kenchinjiru, enjoying the aroma of soy sauce and the sweetness of the root vegetables.

"This is amazing," she said.

She took a bite of the burdock root and carrot.

"This is so delicious. I think that without this cafe, my daily diet would be a total mess."

"I'm glad," Kinoshita said.

Praise seemed to make Kinoshita turn a bit curt, Otoha thought. He must be embarrassed.

"I've hardly ever had kenchinjiru before I came here," Minami said as she sipped the broth. "I knew the name, though."

"Kenchinjiru stew is kind of an odd thing," Tokai explained. "The name's popular, but there are regional differences since in some parts of Japan they make it and in other parts they don't. Part of that might be generational differences, too, though."

He went on. "It's said that kenchinjiru originated as a vegetarian monk dish at the Kenchoji Temple in Kamakura. It was called *kenchojiru*, but the pronunciation changed over time to kenchinjiru. Nowadays it's eaten a lot in Ibaragi and Tochigi Prefectures and those parts of the northern Kanto region. Since they grow a lot of root vegetables and make a lot of konnyaku, which is made from a kind of taro root. I've heard they add udon noodles and make kenchin udon, a popular dish."

"You always know so much, Mr. Tokai," Kinoshita said, impressed.

"Nah—it was on a show on TV the other day."

"Ah, so that explains it, huh?"

"But the fact that Seiko Tanabe made the dish means it spread down to the Kansai region as well, since that's where she's from."

"The main difference, though, is that instead of konnyaku hers uses tofu. You cut up daikon, carrots, burdock, taro, then sauté them in sesame oil, then simmer them in broth, flavor it with soy sauce and lastly add tofu broken into pieces."

"So it's tofu! That's why it has such a gentle taste."

"In Tochigi Prefecture they make kenchinjiru in a huge pot and eat it for several days, then add udon, soba noodles, or rice, to make a kind of porridge. I imagine they don't use tofu since it would fall apart too easily."

"Maybe so."

"I love this kind of set menu the best," Otoha said.

"You said the same thing when I made curry, you know," Kinoshita said and went back into the kitchen.

The sardine dish was cooked sweet and salty and went well with the rice. And when you took a bite of the yukari rice when the somewhat fishy taste still remained in your mouth it was totally refreshing. Otoha felt like she could eat white rice and yukari, switching back and forth between them, forever. The okara had completely absorbed the umami from the cooked sardine broth and was flavorful and tasty. The carrots and dried shiitake provided a pleasant accent.

"I never knew okara was this delicious."

"I know," Tokai agreed. "I didn't like to eat it much when I was a child, but now I think it tastes great."

"In my home," Minami said, "we not only didn't eat kenchinjiru, but we didn't eat okara either."

"Was your family more into Western-style food?"

"I suppose so. We had a lot of stew and hamburgers. My father liked those kinds of dishes."

"He must be young."

"Well, in his fifties. Maybe that's what he's eaten since he was a child."

"Come to mention it, in Mizuki Takashiro's house there was a set of the complete works of Seiko Tanabe."

"Really?"

"I didn't expect that. Tanabe has already passed away and I always felt like much older women read her work."

"Hmm. That might not be the case." Tokai shook his head. "I remember reading somewhere that a girl in her teens who won the Akutagawa Prize said she liked Seiko Tanabe's novels."

"Really? Then maybe age isn't a factor."

"And she wrote about delicious dishes like these. What a great writer!"

Chatting about all kinds of things like this while enjoying dinner was a lot of fun. Otoha felt the exhaustion slowly drain from her body and mind.

EVEN A FEW WEEKS after they went to Mizuki Takashiro's home, they still hadn't organized her collection, which was sitting, untouched, in the meeting room-cum-reception room. Someone proposed they take it for a time to the usual place—that old house on the outskirts of Tokyo, but some felt that with her being such a popular author, putting her books in a place that could easily be broken into wasn't a good idea, so the collection remained packed in boxes in the library. The meeting room was more of a storage room now.

They were still getting a few inquiries and requests from the media, but not as many as right after her passing, and Otoha and the others learned how fleeting people's interest in something could be. They did get a request from a regional bookstore that was going to hold a special festival for Takashiro's books and the booksellers wanted to be allowed to photograph some of them, which led to some debate among the staff. What this bookstore planned was a large panel, featuring a photo of Takashiro's collection on a bookshelf to serve as a backdrop to the festival.

Otoha and her colleagues met to discuss this . . . squeezing into a corner of the meeting room, so filled with her collection that they couldn't set up the table and instead made do with a circle of chairs. Taking the books out of the boxes was, practically speaking, difficult at this point and it seemed too soon, so they decided to turn down the request. Otoha and the others who'd previously worked in bookstores wanted to help out, but the general consensus was that it was still not possible. It felt strange, though, to huddle together discussing this right next to Mizuki Takashiro's enormous collection.

"We're these books' servants, aren't we?" Masako said, and everyone smiled wryly. "Well, that's the right stance for us librarians. To be books' servants."

Masako's voice was low, as if she were speaking to herself alone.

On that day Otoha went back downstairs after eating, and she found Sasai, holding a book, talking with Minami.

Both were frowning, and Otoha suddenly realized what was going on.

Sasai said, "We found another one, Otoha-chan."

"Another one?" she asked.

As she got closer, she realized her intuition was right. Sasai silently opened the inside back cover of the book he was holding. There was nothing stamped there.

"Oh dear."

Since that first time, they'd found more and more books that lacked a collection stamp. At first about one per week, and more recently one every couple of days. If they checked each and every volume there would no doubt be even more.

"How did you notice it?"

"This one's brand-new, just published," Minami said, and Sasai showed her the back cover.

"You're right."

The book was a collection of essays by a famous elderly writer, about his experiences with Tai Chi Chuan and how it dramatically changed his health. It had come out a few months ago and was still a bestseller.

"Just looking at the back cover clued me in. Pretty unusual for such a new book to be here, and one that isn't a novel either. And I don't ever remember seeing it."

"I see."

The three of them sighed in unison.

If that many books had snuck onto the shelves that weren't a part of the specific collections, then that limited the number of potential culprits. There weren't so many people who come here regularly.

First there was the staff, a possibility no one really wanted to consider, though it was hard to deny it completely. And then there were the monthly, and yearly, pass holders.

There were people with monthly passes, though no one had purchased one in the months since they'd first discovered a book missing a collection stamp.

At present there were five or six yearly pass holders. Konosuke Takaki's lover, Kimiko Ninomiya, was one of them, with the rest being a university professor and grad student, students writing theses, and a freelance nonfiction writer working on the poet Mitsuyasu Ando, who died young.

"Like they say, *Search seven times before you start suspecting anyone*," Sasai murmured.

"What's that?" Minami asked.

"Just an old saying. That it's best to be on solid ground before you accuse anyone of being a thief."

"I see."

"Which means we need to do an internal search first."

This had actually come up at a staff meeting not long ago. Looking very reluctant, Sasai had told them, "I'm not saying I suspect any of you, but if anyone knows anything about this, or has some idea, please come forward. If it's hard to say it here in front of everyone, we can talk privately." They all looked at each other and shook their heads.

After this, it seemed no one came forward to talk with Sasai.

"I think I'll ask them too," Sasai said.

"Ask who?" Minami asked.

"The yearly pass holders. The ones who've been here recently. We did our last inventory four months ago, so it'd be the ones who've come frequently since then."

"What'll you ask?" Minami's questions came fast and furious.

"Good question. Not that we suspect them . . . I don't really want to suspect anyone . . . but I just want to explain the situation and ask them if they know anything."

"Will asking that reveal the culprit? You really think they'd confess that? That *I'm the one who did it*?" Minami asked.

"No, I sort of doubt it, but if we merely warn them, let them know we know what's going on, they might quit. Also, I'll tell them we're consulting with Mr. Kuroiwa, a former police officer."

"I get it," Minami said.

"If, after that, they don't stop, though I don't really want to do this, let's push up the collection sorting! If we do that, and we find a book afterward, we'll know it's someone who came to the library after that."

"Whoa," Minami said, grimacing.

"We have no choice."

"I know. It's just that reordering the collection is so much work!"

"Is it really that hard?" Otoha interjected.

"They do inventories at bookstores, right?" Minami asked. "It's the same."

"I see."

"A library's even more work. You have to close for a whole week."

"And we're getting more and more collections—Mr. Shirakawa's, and Ms. Takashiro's, and to make matters worse have put a halt to sorting them. Now on top of that a library-wide inventory."

"I think we have to, though."

"I suppose you're right."

"I, uh—well actually . . ." Minami began, her voice low. "I didn't want to say this, but I've been thinking for a long time that ___-san's been acting kind of suspicious."

Otoha couldn't catch the name.

"Eh?"

She asked again, and Minami breathed in, about to repeat it when Sasai interrupted.

"Let's go inside."

He took Minami by the arm, unusually forcefully, and they went into the staff room behind the reception desk. Otoha glanced around to make sure there were no patrons around and rang the bell on the reception desk, one they rang when someone entered the library or when they had to step away from reception for a while. *Chin chin!* it rang out twice, and then she followed Sasai and Minami into the staff room.

"It's not a good idea to mention patrons' names there," Sasai said. "Even though nobody else is there now . . ."

"I'm sorry," Minami said.

"Why didn't we notice that up till now?" Otoha asked.

"Notice what?" Sasai asked, turning around to look at Otoha.

"The ticket counter outside. Doesn't Mai Kitazato from the front desk check the patrons' bags when they come in and out?"

"True."

"So she'd notice if anyone is leaving a book here," said Otoha. "Since they wouldn't have it when they left."

"We already checked this, didn't we? Ms. Kitazato said no one did that," Sasai replied.

"That's right, but the books were all pocket-size paperbacks. Say they were in a little pouch, for instance, inside an oversized handbag. Even a woman isn't going to open and check out another woman's pouch. And a paperback could be hidden in a person's clothes, too, and we can't do anything about that."

"True. Oh..." As Otoha was speaking, Sasai, his voice rising, raised the book in his hands. "But this is a hardbound, and a brand-new one."

"In that case Ms. Kitazato must have noticed it."

"I would think so."

"Let's go ask her," Otoha said.

The three of them set off to the ticket counter. When they exited the staff room, they found Tokai seated at the reception desk.

EPISODE FOUR

"Ah, thank you, Mr. Tokai."

"Did something happen?" Tokai asked, surprised, perhaps, to see them troop out of the staff room. Not just the three of them together, but all three were running.

"I'll explain later!"

Sasai didn't caution them this time that *Ladies don't run*.

As she headed to the ticket counter, Otoha had the feeling that she had indeed picked up on the name that Minami had murmured earlier. The name of an elderly lady who visited the library almost every day.

Since Otoha had, for some reason, been suspicious of her herself.

Ms. Kitazato looked at that newly published book and listened to Sasai's explanation, and tilted her head in puzzlement. As always, her silky hair spilled down with her movements.

"It's Kimiko Ninomiya's book, isn't it," she said.

"You sure?"

"I'm sure. I remember thinking, 'Ah, so a person like her reads this sort of book, too?' I was struck that even someone like her is careful about her health."

"I see." Sasai sighed, the expression *shoulders drooping* fitting him to a T.

"I was really hoping it wouldn't be her," he said.

Meaning he might have been suspecting her as well.

"What do you mean by *someone like her*?" Otoha asked Kitazato.

"Someone like her?"

"You said Ms. Ninomiya was that kind of person."

"Yeah. I sometimes chat with her when she comes through here."

Otoha found it hard to picture Kitazato talking with patrons any more than was necessary. Maybe Ms. Ninomiya did all the talking.

"She often says she'd like to die quickly, keel over and not linger."

"Huh? She says that, really?"

"I don't know how serious she is, though."

"Maybe it's a joke."

"Could be. There's one more thing that I was concerned about," Kitazato said, and took the book from Sasai.

"I wonder if it's still here," she murmured to herself. She flipped through the pages of the book and found a thin strip of paper there.

"A sales slip!" Otoha couldn't help but shout. New books always had an informational price slip inside.

"At the time I thought, huh, the sales slip's still inside," Kitazato said.

"So this book was shoplifted?" Minami dared ask.

"Large bookstores these days have everything digitalized," Otoha pointed out, "so even if the slip's still inside it doesn't necessarily mean it's been stolen."

"And books ordered online still have the sales slip inside," Minami said. "But for bookstores around here that have digitalized inventory, you'd have to travel to Shinjuku or Ikebukuro in the city, or Hachioji or Tokorozawa in the suburbs."

"Kind of a delicate issue, isn't it."

"Whether it's been shoplifted or not is a secondary, or even tertiary, issue," interjected Sasai. "First of all, we need to ask her about this book . . ."

"I'm sorry about this," Kitazato apologized. "I didn't notice at all . . . Ms. Ninomiya had the book in her bag when she came in, but I didn't notice it wasn't there when she left. Because I'm always worried about *our* books being taken out of here."

"It's like that saying from feudal times, *Keep weapons out, and women in.* You don't worry about a woman coming in when your concern is one of them going out." Minami teased her with this, hoping to make her feel better.

"But that saying doesn't really apply, does it?" Otoha said, and she and Minami laughed.

"Ah, I guess I should go talk to Ms. Ninomiya, shouldn't I . . ." In contrast to their lighter mood, Sasai again let out a deep sigh.

"Shall I go with you?" Otoha, noticing his concern, couldn't help volunteering. Sasai seemed quite depressed about the situation. He always went about his work briskly, efficiently, but with this kind of incident . . . He might not be good when it came to scolding people and warning them about their behavior.

"Are you sure?" he asked.

"In the bookstore I worked at I caught a few shoplifters and had to caution them. Actually, our store was in a shopping mall, and they hired security to handle those shoplifters, but I helped them take care of it, so I understand situations like this."

"But this isn't a case of shoplifting," Minami said, in a teasing tone again. She seemed to be enjoying this, as if the problem was already taken care of. "In fact, the number of our book holdings has increased."

"Very true," Otoha said.

"Which is exactly why it's hard to talk to her," added Sasai. "I don't know what to say to caution her . . ."

"You could have Mr. Kuroiwa come with you. But wouldn't it be good to have another woman there?" Kitazato wondered.

"It would. However, having Mr. Kuroiwa with us would seem like an overreaction, and I'd feel sorry for Ms. Ninomiya." Sasai let out yet another drawn-out sigh.

"Which is why I said I'll go with you."

Sasai, always so steady and in charge, looked so

pained by the prospect that Otoha felt about ready to give him an encouraging slap on the back.

Probably, Otoha mused, a person like him must not handle things well when others acted maliciously—though of course in this case, they didn't know Ms. Ninomiya's motives.

"Yes, it was me," Ms. Ninomiya readily confessed.

"Eh?" She'd so freely admitted it that Sasai repeated the question.

"Yes, that was me."

"You're the one who placed the books there?"

"Indeed I did."

"Was it maybe—by mistake? Like you forgot them there?"

"No." Ms. Ninomiya shook her head. "I placed them there myself. The books without any collection stamps."

Her confession could not have been clearer.

Tonight she was wearing the red coat again. With her slender figure, it looked good on her. Her white hair was done up neatly, and she wore a necklace of large pastel-colored beads. Not expensive jewelry, apparently, but for that very reason it looked good on her and left the impression that she had good taste.

They were in front of the shelves housing Konosuke Takagi's books. Sasai had planned to talk with her in the meeting room-cum-reception room, but when he saw her seated there, reading, he said, "Let's talk here."

There were no other patrons around, and Otoha got the sense that Ms. Ninomiya could be more open and honest here, in front of her late lover's books.

"Well, now . . ." Sasai avoided looking her in the eye. He'd come here trying to get her to confess, but he seemed the most perplexed himself, so Otoha took over.

"We've discovered books like these, up to and including your present one, over the past few months . . . Did you commit this crime?"

At this Ms. Ninomiya's neatly shaped, thin eyebrows shot up.

Where have I seen eyebrows like this before? Otoha thought. *Oh, right—they're like Scarlett O'Hara's in the old movie.*

"Crime? I suppose so . . . As long as there's no one else who's been doing this."

Otoha and Sasai exchanged a glance.

"Before it was Dazai paperbacks," Sasai said.

"Ah, then it was me."

"I see." Sasai nodded heavily.

"Why did you do it?"

Ms. Ninomiya put the book she'd been reading on her lap . . . It was from Kosuke Takagi's collection,

Robert B. Parker's novel *Early Autumn* . . . She closed her eyes, gave it some thought, then spoke.

"I had no other place to put them," she said.

"No other place?" Otoha and Sasai both asked.

"My apartment is quite small and I have no room to keep all the books."

"Ah, so that's the reason."

Sasai let out a small sigh. He seemed relieved. Her actions weren't a crime, or malicious, but had a rational explanation . . . though it was hard to say if those actions were normal, to stealthily put her books in their library just because they wouldn't fit in her apartment. Sasai found that easier to accept—that an old woman would place books with no collection stamp in the library not out of maliciousness, to deliberately cause confusion, but simply because she was stuck for a solution.

"That being the case, you should have told us beforehand. If you'd said you'd like to donate some books, we could have handled that."

"Then you would put my books next to Papa Takagi's?"

"No, that would be . . . No, we couldn't. I'm sorry, but we wouldn't be able to put them in the library. But we would help you find someone to take them or dispose of them."

"I thought so, that you'd take them away somewhere," she said. "I don't want that to happen."

"Okay . . . but the thing is . . ."

"My books want to be *here* forever, too."

Oh boy, Otoha told herself. *Another sticky situation. We only keep authors' collections here. We can't go storing an old woman's collection of books. Though getting her to accept that might be next to impossible.*

Sasai was silent so Otoha asked, "Do you have that many books in your place, Ms. Ninomiya? You must be quite the reader."

She threw this out there, without much thought, as a change of topic.

"Not at all. I'm no great reader. Compared to Papa Takagi. I just read a bit. But I do have a lot of books I took away from bookstores."

Took away?

Otoha and Sasai looked at each other.

Took away could be interpreted in two different ways.

If it meant stealing, then that would explain the book with the sales slip still in it.

"You took that book from a bookstore?"

"That's right," Ms. Ninomiya said lightly.

Otoha and Sasai were speechless, and Ms. Ninomiya, looking at their faces, laughed loudly.

"That surprises you? Shoplifting books isn't a crime. Like they say—*It's no crime to steal flowers*. It's the same thing. Books are supposed to be passed around. That's

EPISODE FOUR

okay, since we learn things from reading books, and return that knowledge to society."

Otoha was too flabbergasted to speak.

She had heard something about this from staff at the bookstore she used to work at, that among the elite class before the war, there were people who felt that way. And old novels had scenes where affluent students shoplifted from bookstores.

Values change with the times. Still, this was a shock. Blithely thinking it was okay to shoplift . . . as if insisting they had a *right* to do so?

Ms. Ninomiya laughed all the more. "Is this too intense for young people now, I wonder? But it's true. Papa Takagi said so."

"Takagi said that? . . . I mean, *Mister* Takagi actually said that?" Otoha asked.

While he was still alive, many times Otoha had helped at the bookstore with special bookfairs devoted to his works and displaying Takagi's books out on the shelves. She'd written dozens of the handwritten little point-of-purchase ads for them, the kind they'd place next to the books to draw the customers' attention, but now she felt like ripping those all to shreds.

"That's right. In the past, talented people like Papa Takagi used to say that."

So what did she think a bookstore was? Didn't she

realize how many books they'd have to sell to recover the cost of one stolen? Otoha took a deep breath, about to lash out at her, but right as she opened her mouth Sasai lightly took her by the arm. She looked up and saw him shake his head slightly, which she took as a sign that she should stifle her feelings. She calmed down and finally exhaled. Instead, tears now welled up in her eyes.

"Among the books you shelved here—I mean, other than this one—they were all used books, weren't they? These books were all stolen as well?"

"That's right," Ms. Ninomiya said. "I used to steal them from used bookstores right near here. When Papa Takagi was still alive, we'd go together sometimes. But these days none of the stores will let me in, so I changed to bookshops that sell new books."

So the used bookstores found out what she was doing and banned her . . . Otoha realized this with a start, and asked, nervously, "Have you, by any chance, also stolen books from us?"

If she had no remorse over stealing that many books, it wouldn't be strange for her to steal some from the library. They hadn't found any had been missing, but perhaps there had been a few that escaped their notice.

"There's no way I'd steal any." Ms. Ninomiya's strongly denied it. "I mean, these are Papa Takagi's precious books. If I stole them, it would makes things hard for his fans. His fans are important."

Beside her, Sasai breathed out in relief. He seemed greatly comforted to hear that.

"But what about other people's books?"

"Other people's? Other writers' collections? I'm not going to steal those. I find no interest or value in books other than Papa Takagi's."

"I'm glad," Otoha couldn't help but say.

She could be lying, of course (since she had actually stolen other writers' books from used and new bookstores), but Otoha felt like her strong denial here could, to some extent, be believed.

"Other writers are all junk," Ms. Ninomiya went on muttering, as if to herself. "I may be old, but Kimiko Ninomiya is not about to steal books with other writers' seals stamped in them."

Otoha found her insistence made sense. Or did it?

At any rate, they couldn't allow her in the library again. But Otoha had no idea how they should convey that to her, what they should do. If she could only consult with Masako and Ako about this . . . if all the library staff, Mai Kitazato from the front desk and Detective Kuroiwa included, could discuss it, things would work out.

The thought encouraged her.

"Ms. Ninomiya, were you . . . Mr. Takagi's . . . girlfriend?"

Saying *lover* would be rude, she figured, so she chose that term instead.

"That's right."

"I heard that's why you come so often to the library. Someone told me that . . ."

"So what about it?" Ms. Ninomiya frowned angrily, her tone clearly belligerent.

"I heard that you wanted to be close to Mr. Takagi's books. Do you spend your time just reading his books? What about others?"

She asked this to soothe Ms. Ninomiya's feelings by shifting the topic, and also to know more about how she spent her time here, since that might make it easier in the future for them to locate books missing collection stamps.

"That's right."

The question wasn't that deep or probing, yet for an instant, just an instant, Ms. Ninomiya silently looked at her, blinking her eyes in thought.

Why this uncomfortable feeling? Otoha wondered . . . *I don't understand why, but I feel like I've annoyed her.*

"That's not it, is it," Sasai said in a low voice.

"Eh?"

This from Otoha, who was more surprised than Ms. Ninomiya that Sasai had spoken up.

"I don't think that's right. Wanting to be near his books isn't the only reason you come here."

"What are you talking about?"

"Of course you want to be near his books. But that simple reason is not the whole story. I've known the reason for quite some time. It didn't bother me, though, so I didn't say anything."

"What do you mean, Mr. Sasai?" Otoha asked.

"I didn't say anything to anyone because I figured it was a question of privacy. But I can't allow the library to be besmirched in this way. Having books without collection stamps, and stolen books to boot, placed here is unacceptable."

Sasai shot Otoha a glance.

"The only other person here is a staff member, Ms. Higuchi, so I will go ahead and say this. Is that okay? I know you've been searching all this time for one book in particular of Mr. Takagi's."

Ms. Ninomiya lowered her eyes. That could be taken as either a yes or a no. She neither answered back or resisted. Her body, though, suddenly seemed to have shrunk one whole size.

"I noticed what you've been doing," Sasai continued. "While you're here you're always secretly looking at a letter as you try to locate a book. An old letter. If anyone else comes in here you hurriedly put it away. I figured it must be a very precious, secret letter. I've watched you sometimes from a distance, so you haven't noticed. It's less that you're reading the letter than comparing it to the books. I concluded that this is a book cipher, and you're looking for the book that holds the key."

Ms. Ninomiya didn't reply.

"A book cipher?" Otoha asked.

"A code where a book or some writing serves as the key to decoding it," Sasai explained. "The people exchanging this have to have the same edition of the same book. Anyone else has to search through countless books. Even, for instance, if you lost the key you can find it again. It's a classic, but quite handy form of sending secret messages."

"I had no idea," Otoha said.

"The letter contains numbers that point to certain page numbers and lines, and to the number word or letter in a line."

"To someone who doesn't know that, then, it's just a letter full of numbers?"

"Correct. Somehow, Ms. Ninomiya, you got hold of a letter written in code to, well, one would imagine it to be someone with a relationship with Mr. Takagi, right? And you came here to decipher it. Normally you wouldn't think the letter was written to his wife. If it were his wife who he's living with, there wouldn't be any need to exchange a code, would there."

Ms. Ninomiya remained silent, eyes down.

"Who did he write the letter to?" Sasai asked.

No response.

"Well, that's okay. Honestly, that fact itself has nothing to do with us. But I was thinking that maybe you'd already deciphered the book cipher."

Ms. Ninomiya, showing no reaction till now, looked up, startled.

"Why do you think that?" she asked.

"Because you've been coming here for several years. You must have looked into all of Mr. Takagi's books and investigated every volume, haven't you? And if you were his lover, and close to him, you must have had some idea. That Mr. Takagi would choose a book he was particularly fond of, or one he often read, a book that he had some sort of feelings for."

Ms. Ninomiya was silent for a while, then suddenly burst out laughing. Sasai and Otoha looked at each other, afraid that maybe the woman had suddenly gone soft in the head.

After her outburst of laughter, she replied, "That wasn't the case."

"It wasn't?"

"It took me so much time. Since it was the very last book I examined."

"The very last one?"

"I figured that book couldn't be it, so I put off looking at it. So it took a long time to decipher it."

"Is that right. Not a book Mr. Takagi was fond of?"

"No, the opposite. The book I thought he liked the best, the one he was most fond of . . . A book I gave him. Actually, one I told him about. 'This is a good book,' I said, 'I recommend it. You should read it.' That turned out to be the key."

"Which book was it?"

This was less part of the interrogation than curiosity on Otoha's part.

"Saneatsu Mushanokoji's *Love and Death*."

"Ah."

Sasai quickly nodded, but Otoha had never read it.

"A short book like that?"

"Um. It was long enough, since the letter was just about how he loved that other woman, how he was willing to die for her. I couldn't stand it anymore, so I took the book home and threw it away. And replaced it."

"With the Osamu Dazai book."

"Yes. I happened to have it with me, and it was about the same thickness."

So that's how she started to place books here.

"So you did steal a book from here, didn't you?"

"No. Because I gave him that book. It's *my* book."

"What do you mean?"

"He used the book to write the encoded letter to his new lover . . . After Papa Takagi's wife passed away, even though he and I were basically living together."

Even if he did it as a joke, he was an awful man to do that—to use a book his lover had given as the key for a coded letter to another lover. No, maybe that's exactly *why* he chose that book, so no one would notice.

"Okay, but why did you keep coming here even after you decoded the cipher? You didn't need to, did you?"

Sasai was rather harsh this evening, doing a brilliant job of interrupting her words. Though Ms. Ninomiya had opened her mouth and seemed to want to say even more.

Maybe she wanted us to hear what she had to say, Otoha thought. Her complaints and reminiscences. But Sasai would have none of it.

"Because I was lonely and had nowhere else to go. If I come here there are books, and young people."

Otoha unconsciously looked away.

So that's it—*she had nowhere else to go.* Being here helped her pass the long, lonely hours of the night.

For so long she'd been the lover of a married man, had shoplifted books, and had no family of her own.

And tonight she no doubt would lose that place, her one refuge, forever.

FINAL EPISODE

YOKO MORI'S CANNED FOOD RECIPES

After the incident with Kimiko Ninomiya, the Night Library was closed for a long time.

Sasai made a proposal, which the staff members discussed a few times, deciding first of all to use the first three weeks to do a full inventory of the library's holdings, after which the whole staff were to take time off. The owner would get in touch with Sasai ahead of time when the library was to be reopened. Sasai explained that this would probably be, at most, a month. The lengthy break was, as he explained, "So that everyone can recover from doing the inventory, and so that the owner can check the library." The owner promised that during this time they would all continue to receive their usual salaries.

And so, very quietly, the Night Library shut its doors to the world . . .

At least it felt that way to Otoha.

Naturally researchers and writers contacted them one after the other, wanting to continue to use the library. Sasai refunded the monthly pass holders, telling them they would carefully respond to any requests for information through email and so on, thus persuading them to accept the sudden closing.

They also discussed their working hours during the collection inventory period, deciding they would continue with the 4:00 p.m. to 1:00 a.m. schedule. Some felt that since there were no patrons during this time it might be best to go with a 9:00 a.m. to 6:00 p.m. schedule, but Masako's opinion won the day—that since they were all used to working at night, changing to a normal schedule for over a month and then trying to return to a night schedule would prove difficult.

Their in-house detective, Mr. Kuroiwa, plus Mai Kitazato at reception, and Mr. Kinoshita were allowed to come to work or take time off, whichever they wished. Kuroiwa and Kinoshita elected to take time off.

"Ever since I retired I've never had this much time off," Mr. Kuroiwa said, "and I've decided to go on a trip with my wife. Our son lives in Hokkaido and I was thinking we'd go visit him." When Mr. Kuroiwa said this at a meeting he was summoned to, there was a subdued stir among the others. *So Mr. Kuroiwa has a wife . . . and a family*, Otoha thought, and the staff members must have felt pretty much the same.

Kinoshita didn't explain his reasons for choosing time off. Which was in keeping with his personality.

Ms. Kitazato decided to come to work.

"I'd like to come to work the same as everyone else. I have to lock and unlock the front door, and if there are things I can do to help with the inventory, I will."

Otoha found this unexpected. She hadn't figured that Kitazato, always so cool and aloof, would choose to work alongside everyone else.

They decided unanimously that Masako, with a long career as a librarian, would be manager during this time. She was appointed to that position, and with her recommendation Minami appointed as assistant manager. And under Masako's leadership and direction the collection inventory commenced. They'd done inventories before, but it was a new experience for Otoha and Tokuda, so the process was carefully explained to them.

"All libraries conduct an inventory about once a year," Masako told them the first day. "It's nothing unusual, but it's very important work. We have to make sure all the books are in their proper places so we can quickly and accurately respond to patron's requests, and provide them with the proper books. I expect we may find some books missing, and outside books mixed in."

Masako gazed around at them all.

"Honestly it won't be hard to check lost books, since if we check data and documents related to our holdings, those should pop up on their own . . . But books on the shelves from outside is not something that happens very much with libraries, so we need to pay careful attention."

"To do that we'll assign two of you to each author, and both of you will compare our records with what's actually on the shelves. When you're done, you'll once again do a count of the volumes in each author's collection and compare it with our database." Minami, standing beside Masako, said this in a loud voice. Perhaps she was tense, for her voice was a bit raspy, her face flushed.

"And, uh . . . and besides the ones who first check a collection, please have several other staff members recheck the numbers."

Minami cleared her throat to get her voice back to normal. "Thank you all in advance," she said.

The explanation over, Minami and Masako bowed to the group, which responded with applause.

FINAL EPISODE

ONCE THEY STARTED, IT wasn't such a bad time. At least Otoha thought so. They'd come to work at 4:00 p.m., check the holdings in groups of two, counting the number of volumes. The first teams consisted of Masako and Ako, Minami and Otoha, Sasai and Tokuda, and Tokai and Kitazato, and then after a few days they would switch partners.

"If we keep the same teams, you'll get too used to being together, and that might increase the risk of mistakes," Masako explained.

Masako and the others figured that, for the books with only collections stamps in them, and no call numbers or bar codes, it would take twice as long to sort them as in a normal library.

"In ordinary libraries, including organizing the closed stacks, they usually do about one third of their holdings once a year. Meaning their schedule is to check the entire collection every three years. But we're going to be doing it all in one fell swoop."

On their days off, they gathered in Minami's room and watched the sequels to the drama *Anne of Green Gables*. Otoha wished those times could last forever.

During this closure, only Otoha and Sasai went to meet people outside the library.

They talked with Mizuki Takashiro's younger sister again, needing to decide on a design for the collections stamp. She got in touch with them, saying she was moving from that high-rise condo and downsizing her belongings, and wanted them to come see her before all that took place. She didn't state this clearly, but Sasai said it sounded like she might be moving away from the Kanto area.

Around noon on the day Takashiro's younger sister designated, Otoha visited the high-rise condo with Sasai. They wouldn't be transporting any books this time, so they took a couple of trains to the high-rises in Musashi-Kosugi.

They barely spoke in the train, but it didn't feel stifling or uncomfortable to Otoha. Ever since they'd finished up the Kimiko Ninomiya incident, she felt the others had become not just colleagues but something more—there was a sense of solidarity with them akin to that of a family or siblings.

Perhaps, though, she was the only one feeling that way. She had no way of confirming this with Sasai, a thought that left her a little sad.

Mizuki Takashiro's apartment was still and quiet, the younger sister, who asked to be called Mone, was dressed in sweatpants and was her usual disinterested self. Like before, she led them into the living room.

Now that the collection was gone, the bookshelves lay empty. You would think with all the books removed they would look neat and tidy, but when a huge bookshelf lacked a single book and the room was dirty, the impression was that a thief had just come and gone.

Sasai showed her the design mockups for the collection stamp he'd had prepared. If she didn't have any particular wishes one way or the other, he had several miniature specimens displaying the author's full name. The only three choices to be decided on were whether the writing in the carved stamp would be raised against a carved-out background (or the opposite), the question of whether they would use vertical or horizontal writing, and the choice of font.

"None of them really grabs me," the sister said after taking a look.

"This one is the simplest design," Sasai explained. "If you have a design or picture you like, we can include that. For example, you could add an illustration of an object the late author was fond of." Sasai quickly seized the opportunity to make this suggestion, and the sister tilted her head, considering it.

"No, nothing in particular . . ." she drawled.

Otoha, silent until then, interjected, "Once we stamp it, that's it, it can't be changed. So you don't want to have any regrets . . ."

"Regrets?"

As expected, Mone shot her a dubious glance. Deep frown lines appeared between her eyebrows, and though she flinched, Otoha dared to forge on and added, "Many times when our patrons pick up a book, they open the back cover and check out the stamp. These stamps have a great influence on the impression one gets of a book and author . . ."

She expected the sister to have a comeback like *Who cares? I'm not interested*, but surprisingly she nodded seriously. "I see," she said.

"Everyone's happy to see stamps that remind them of the author back when they were alive."

"Well, Mizuki liked books, for one thing . . . Not that that's anything special. Being a writer and all . . ."

"We could make a book design incorporating the author's name," Sasai explained.

"Really?"

Sasai quickly sketched a picture of a book next to the simple stamp design. On the cover of the book he wrote *Mizuki Takashiro*.

"Not the best drawing, but you get the idea."

"Hmm . . ." Mone studied it.

"What do you think? If there are other things the author liked, particular flowers or fruits or animal, for instance we can use those."

"Mizuki liked cats . . . Though was allergic to them and couldn't have any."

"Cats? Of course we can add a cat to the design. I'd have to check with the designer, so after I take it back shall I text you the design?"

"Can you make it like Soseki Natsume's book?"

"You mean the first edition of *I Am a Cat*?"

"No, not the famous naked half cat, half human figure, but the gold leaf and orange drawing at the bottom of the cover . . ."

"Ah, yes that's pretty and cute, isn't it."

While Mone and Sasai's conversation continued, Otoha did a search for the first edition of *I Am a Cat* on her cell phone and came up with the image.

"Yes, that sort of idea." Mone nodded at the screen Otoha held up to her.

"Should we make the font similar?" Otoha asked, pointing to the rounded writing of the cover.

"That might be good."

"I'll check with the designer about it," Otoha said.

Mone nodded happily. The nicest expression they'd ever seen from her.

Which led Otoha to blurt out, "May I ask you something?"

"What?"

Mone's tone up to this point wasn't so severe. It was like she'd let her guard down and could be honest and open. Sasai looked over worriedly at Otoha, but she decided she'd plunge on.

"When we came here the last time we talked about cleaning the toilet, remember? You told me women shouldn't be expected to clean toilets."

"Did I?"

"Is that something you heard from Mizuki Takashiro?"

"Hmm . . . did I?" she mumbled. Otoha stared fixedly at her, so as not miss a single nuance of her expression.

"Was that Takashiro's idea?"

"Why do you say that?"

"Because it sounds so much like something Takashiro would say."

Otoha was careful not to call her *Takapon*.

"Not all my ideas are influenced by that person you know."

"But one of Takashiro's early blogs uses the same words."

"Then it's just a coincidence."

"Is that right?"

"'Cause we're completely different people," Mone declared.

SASAI AND OTOHA LEFT the apartment together. They were in the building elevator when Otoha said, "I wonder if Mone-san and Takapon really were on such bad terms. Sometimes . . . I don't feel like it."

Sasai tilted his head as if taken by surprise. "Really?" he asked.

"Maybe they were really close, or else their way of thinking was very similar."

"Huh?" Sasai said.

"Other than in the literary works, Takapon never ever wrote about personal ideas in essays or on social networking. However, as I mentioned earlier, Takapon was writing a work that was online, in the very, very early days of Takapon's career, and for a very short time wrote a blog linked to the online novel. Since that's how you pull people in and increase access to online novels . . . But Takapon soon became really popular and quit doing that."

"Huh."

"It was literally just a few weeks. But someone took screenshots of those, and part of that made its way around the internet."

"Interesting."

"Like I said before, Mone said the same thing to me that was online in that blog. The comment about cleaning toilets. 'They put you on toilet duty since you're a woman?' The same thing that Mone said to me. That in some other countries cleaning toilets is considered work for women and slaves. That really upset Mizuki Takashiro. To think that women were considered lower than terrorist criminals."

"Even so, Mone denied it so flatly, it seems, conversely, kind of suspicious. She didn't have to deny it *that* strongly."

We're completely different people . . . It's obvious to anyone that they were, but still . . . Otoha murmured.

"She's the younger sister," Sasai said, "so maybe that's why she thinks the same way and says the same things. Maybe the younger sister read that blog post and agreed with the posted observations."

Sasai sounded like he was soothing Otoha.

"I can picture that with things that are written in the novels," Otoha said, "but would their thinking on something small like that in the blogs be the same? I mean, she disliked her sibling enough to want to get rid of all the possessions quickly and get money out of it."

"The closer people are, the more complex the emotions they have."

"I guess so . . . but still . . ."

Here the elevator reached the first floor.

Otoha didn't let it go even after they'd exited the building.

"I'm sorry, but I just find it hard to believe. Is Mizuki Takashiro really dead?"

"I believe so," Sasai said. "I didn't see Takashiro personally after the death, of course, or check the death certificate myself. But if Takashiro wasn't dead those big newspapers wouldn't publish obituaries, and publishing houses wouldn't print articles about it, would they?"

"I suppose so . . ."

"Plus what's the point to faking her death? If she wanted to quit being a novelist, she could stop for a while, or retire completely."

"I know."

Otoha's head drooped as she followed after Sasai.

"What do you really think, Ms. Higuchi . . . about the relationship between Mizuki Takashiro and the younger sister?" Sasai asked this after a while, on the way to Musashi-Kosugi station. His voice was gentle, and it was less an actual question than him trying to lend an ear and help her figure out her feelings.

"I was thinking. . . . that the person known as Mizuki Takashiro is really . . . the younger sister."

"I see . . ." Sasai nodded, noncommittal.

"Yet it's like you said, that they wouldn't announce a death if someone hasn't actually died. I don't know how these things work, but if by any chance word got out that they'd spread the information that the person had died even though they hadn't, not just that person would come under fire, but the publishing firm too."

"I would think so."

"But imagine if two writers were using one pen name? . . . Dividing up the work? . . . Maybe that's not the case here, though Mizuki Takashiro was famous for writing in so many different genres."

"I see."

"So say one of them died and an obituary is published, that would put an abrupt end to the writing career of Mizuki Takashiro," Otoha said.

"That's not out of the realm of possibility. But after building up the Takashiro brand, so to speak, it would be a waste to just throw it away. But my way of thinking, as an ordinary person, must be very different from that of a genius like Takashiro."

"Goodness," Otoha said.

"Getting rid of the entire collection is kind of a waste. There's no need to go that far."

"I suppose so . . . but what if she wanted to get a completely fresh start?"

"It's odd that her younger sister would have that much anger toward something inside her."

"Maybe she's playacting?"

"I found her anger genuine," Sasai said. "If I suddenly lost someone I loved, I think I too might not just be sad, but angry too."

"I suppose so."

Otoha found it unexpected for Sasai to use the words *someone I loved*, and wondered whether such a person existed for him, someone he loved so much he'd get angry at their loss. As they spoke, they arrived at the station and Sasai bought their tickets. "I can list this as a business expense," he said.

"If you want that much for her to still be alive, Ms. Higuchi . . ." Sasai said, turning around on the escalator to look at Otoha. "Then why don't you think of Takashiro as still alive inside you?" he added.

"Still alive?"

"You're free to believe that. It was announced that she was dead, but you're free to believe she's still alive. That she's alive somewhere and may someday publish another novel."

Otoha recalled the high-rise condo they'd just left. The very top floor felt so very far away now.

"Is it alright to think that way?"

"Of course. Think whatever way you like. We're free to do so."

Otoha felt better, albeit only slightly.

"Thank you so much for saying that," she said, words of gratitude spilling out.

"How come?" Sasai looked at her curiously.

"I feel so encouraged by you."

"Really? Then I'm glad."

"Your words have always helped me, Mr. Sasai. Ever since I first came here."

"Huh?" Sasai, hanging onto the strap in the train, was surprised. "That's the first time anyone's ever said that to me."

"Really? I think everyone feels that way."

"I'm grateful. I never thought I was of much use to other people," Sasai said.

"Now *that's* surprising. I really love what you say to us."

Otoha surprised herself, using the word *love* here, though of course it was limited in scope to a colleague. *Yikes*, she thought, her face growing red, and she gazed downward. Sasai, too, might be feeling something, as he remained silent.

After a few more stations she looked up at him, and it felt—perhaps because the sunlight was striking him—that he, too, was blushing.

"Can I ask you one more thing?" Otoha said.

"What is it?"

"The long vacation period we'll be getting—how long a period is the owner thinking about?" This had been weighing on Otoha's mind for quite some time.

"As I explained to everyone," Sasai said, "it's best to think of it as from two weeks to, at most, about a month."

Otoha noticed how his tone of voice had suddenly changed, and she couldn't help studying him. These were the kind of perfunctory words he'd say when talking to the whole staff. His face, red and blushing up till a minute ago, had returned to its normal hue. It felt to her like he was hiding something.

Otoha didn't have any ulterior motive in asking, but now she felt, conversely, a little shaken.

"Is the fact that the vacation time isn't set an indication that the owner is considering closing the library permanently?" She asked this, half jokingly, as if to dampen her anxiety.

"No, that's not the case," Sasai said firmly, and a little too quickly. The warm feeling she'd felt they shared had now completely dissipated. His quick denial reminded her of Mizuki Takashiro's younger sister. "So you don't trust the owner, Ms. Higuchi? That's a shame."

This left her even more shaken. Sasai was acting kind of standoffish now, like when she had first started at the library. She hurriedly explained. "No, it's not that I don't trust the owner . . . I was thinking if it's two weeks I'll go back home to see my parents, but if it's a month I'll travel to Cebu Island in the Philippines, do some short-term study abroad, or attend English conversation school to practice the language."

These were only recent, passing thoughts she'd had, but she glossed this over by making it sound like they were long-held desires. She remembered how envious she'd been, in the past, when she read a school friend's Facebook post about how she was attending an English conversation school in Cebu.

But now, explaining it to Sasai like this, she really

did feel as if she'd always wanted to do that.

"I've been to Cebu myself," Sasai said. "Attended a school there, too."

"You did? Really?"

He listed the names of a few schools and explained, in surprising detail, their specialties and levels.

"You know a lot about them."

"I went there to brush up my English before I attended college in the US."

She'd asked how long the break would be, but it felt like they'd gotten sidetracked.

"So if I knew how long our break is going to be . . ." she ventured.

"If that's what's holding you up, I'd say don't worry about it and just go. Even if the break ends while you're there, it's okay if you continue at the school. I'll explain the situation to the owner. I think we'll be able to get you paid time off."

"Th-thank you very much."

It was a strange thing. She'd just been told something she was quite thankful for, yet hearing it only increased her anxiety. It felt like if she asked any more questions she'd get mixed up in something even more frightening.

She barely spoke another word on the way back to the library.

FINAL EPISODE

A WEEK AFTER THEY'D begun inventory of the collections Otoha woke up around noon, and had breakfast—lunch, as most people would call it—as she watched TV. The program was a show she'd recorded the day before, a drama that was half mystery, half love story, with endless scenes where the heroine suspected the man she was falling for might be the actual perpetrator.

"Are you really that dense?" Otoha called out in a small voice to the TV. "He's not the killer—it's the *older brother*!" Just then she heard someone gently knock at the door.

She peeked out the peephole, expecting to see either another resident of the dorm or else a delivery man with a box sent from her parents, but instead she saw a young woman about her age standing there. *Who is this?* she wondered, not opening the door but voicing the question aloud: "Who is it?" The person said something, but she couldn't catch the name. Resigned to it, she opened the door, keeping the chain latched.

The woman had mid-length hair, and was wearing a cardigan and a long skirt, nothing out of the ordinary, but she was quite tall and had a stocky build. Perhaps for that reason she looked quite competent, a leader type. Like, perhaps, a former assistant captain of a sports club.

"I'm sorry, but who are you again?" Otoha asked.

"My name's Iwasaki," the woman said. "I'm a friend of Saho Oda, who used to live here. She left something here, apparently, and I've come to fetch it for her."

"Oh . . ."

Otoha remembered that the day she had moved in there was a cardboard box in the closet and Sasai had told her the former resident would come claim it.

"She said it's a cardboard box . . . a box that used to have tangerines in it."

The size and everything else checked out.

"Yes, it's here alright, but I'd like to check with my supervisor first."

"Of course. I've brought Saho's ID, too, with me."

She showed Otoha a driver's license with a photograph. The woman on it was very gentle looking. She was one year older than Otoha.

"If you turn it over you'll see this address on it. She changed her address but then went back to her hometown."

As she'd said, the address was on the back of the license.

"I see, so she really is Ms. Oda's stand-in here," Sasai said after hearing Otoha's explanation. "I think it's okay to give it to her."

Otoha took the cardboard box out of the closet. She hadn't moved it from then until now. It was disappointingly light, as if there was very little inside.

FINAL EPISODE

"Here you are," she said.

This time she unhooked the chain, opened the door and handed over the box.

"Thank you very much." This Ms. Iwasaki bowed and took the box. "Apparently she has some seasonal clothes inside."

"I see." Otoha nodded, unsure what else to say.

"I appreciate it. Thank you so much." The woman bowed again.

"Okay then . . ."

Otoha was about to close the door but the woman said, "I was wondering . . ."

"Yes?"

"Is there anything strange about this place?"

"Huh?"

Strange? Did she mean the dorm? Or the library? If she meant the library, well then it was true, it was chock-full of odd things.

"Here. This room, I mean."

Clutching the box to her, Iwasaki motioned to the floor with her chin. "Strange? Do you mean the apartment's amenities, or layout of the rooms? Or are you talking about something more . . . ghostly?"

"I don't know if *ghostly* is the right word . . ."

Iwasaki came closer to Otoha and lowered her voice.

"Saho said there's something in this room, something that comes out. She was scared all the time. She said she felt like when she was out, someone was in the room, or had come into the room. One time while working, she forgot something and came back to get it and heard a sound from the room next door."

"Really?".

The room next door probably means Minami's.

"She asked the others in the library, complained about it, but they didn't believe her. Nothing was actually missing so Saho couldn't prove anything. But she was so frightened she quit her job here."

"Is that right . . ."

"She loves books and was happy when she first started working here."

"I haven't noticed anything at all," Otoha said. "And I've never sensed any spirit or anything."

"Really? . . . I guess Saho was just imagining things," Iwasaki said, tilting her head, puzzled. "Maybe because of that she moved out so hurriedly she forget these belongings, but she said she was too frightened to retrieve them herself, so that's why I'm here."

"I see. Well, thank you for that."

"Oh, so it wasn't like she said," Iwasaki murmured, looking a little disappointed when she left. She, too, seemed to not put much stock in what Saho Oda believed.

FINAL EPISODE

THAT DAY WHEN OTOHA went to work she casually, just as a passing thought, really, snapped a photo with her cell phone of the specimen of the moth embedded in the marble wall at the entrance. She passed it nearly every day and was no longer as leery of it as she had been.

"What're you going to do with that?" Kitazato asked. She was seated at the entrance, pretty much the same as when the library was open.

Otoha had hardly ever spoken with her, but once they'd begun the inventory they were paired together once, and they now spoke to each other more. Kitazato was very methodical, had beautiful handwriting, and Otoha knew she was a person who stepped forward when difficult work had to be done.

"I thought I'd look into what this type of moth is called."

"Can you find out?"

"I was thinking of doing an image search."

"Interesting." Kitazato nodded, actually not showing much interest.

Once inside the library Otoha ran a search on the photo she'd taken.

The screen was filled with photos of moths, all of similar lapis lazuli color, which made Otoha flinch. She was used to seeing one here at the library, but still the photo of dozens of moths pasted to a tree trunk made her shudder.

When she found ones that looked close to the one she'd photographed, she tapped them and read the pages with the explanations. But when she looked carefully, their patterning was all slightly different, the size given in the explanations just not a match.

Is it really this hard to pin down? she wondered, about ready to give up when she tapped the final photo and came to a halt.

KOKO KOBAYASHI

The explanation said: "Originally from Malaysia. The scientific name is from, unusually, the name of a Japanese woman. One theory has it this is the name of a woman friend of the person who discovered this moth, Professor Kozo Ida."

Kobayashi . . . She felt like she'd heard that name here before at the library. Did this Kobayashi . . . Koko Kobayashi . . . have some connection with the library?

Otoha stood there and looked up. The ceiling loomed one story above, with bookshelves rising all the way up to it. Were these shelves made by the same *Ms. Kobayashi*?

Ms. Kobayashi, the cleaner for the library?

It was a pretty common last name, though . . .

"Ms. Higuchi."

She turned around, startled. It was Sasai. She felt like she'd been discovered doing something she shouldn't be and hurriedly stuffed her cell phone in her pocket.

"What is it?" she asked.

Her surprise, coupled with a lingering guilty conscience from the incident the other day, made her voice come out sounding aggressive.

"I'm sorry, I saw you just standing there and wondered what was going on," Sasai answered timidly.

"No . . . uh, everything's fine."

"You're sure?"

"Of course."

She forced a smile.

"I'm sorry about a while ago. The thing with Saho Oda," Sasai said.

"It's okay. I just handed over the cardboard box, that's all. But the friend of hers who came to pick it up said something a bit odd."

"Odd?"

"She said Ms. Oda felt some kind of presence in the dorm. Like someone else had come into her room. And that's why she quit."

"Ah." Sasai nodded. "Ms. Oda was a little highly strung, and didn't fit in here . . . I couldn't deal with it as I should have . . . and I regret how things ended up."

"Really?"

"What about you, Otoha?"

"What do you mean?"

It was the first time Sasai had called her by her first name, and it threw her for a moment.

"Is there anything about your room, Otoha, that concerns you?"

"No, not really. Nothing in particular."

"I'm glad."

Sasai smiled broadly and looked at her.

"What I hope is that everyone can enjoy working and living here."

"Right."

She felt like he was lumping her in with *everyone here*, which made her a bit sad.

"If anything ever happens," he said, "please let me know right away . . . Oh, right. Mizuki Takashiro's younger sister got in touch again."

"What did she say?"

"She said she doesn't want to go with the cat design after all, and wants something simple instead."

"Oh."

Otoha found this a bit disappointing, but it seemed somehow more fitting for Takashiro.

"Are you going back to that condo again?" Otoha asked.

"No." Sasai shook his head. "We'll email each other about the design. I understand she's going to sell the place."

"Ah, so she decided to."

Sasai saw how dejected Otoha looked and laughed. "After this collection inventory is finished we'll have to organize Mizuki Takashiro's collection. You and Masako and the others will be very busy."

"Is it okay to put the collection on public display right away?" Otoha asked.

"I think, like with other authors, we can announce it when we've reached Takashiro's place in line. The sister has agreed, and we can all discuss it at some point."

"Okay."

Otoha glanced around her. "Um . . . the cleaning . . . Ms. Kobayashi who always does the cleaning here? What is she doing now?"

"Excuse me?" Sasai looked at Otoha. His face seemed to tense up, or was she overthinking it? "Ms. Kobayashi is off today. Why do you ask?"

"No real reason . . . it's just that I heard already what the others, Mr. Kuroiwa and Mr. Kinoshita, will be doing during their time off, but I realized I hadn't asked about Ms. Kobayashi."

"Ms. Kobayashi talked with me directly. She'll mainly be off but will come in once a week to take care of cleaning."

"I see. Then, uh, there's . . ."

"What is it?"

Otoha was about to ask about the moth specimen but clammed up.

She suddenly remembered how Sasai had told her that searching for the owner's identity would only invite less than desirable consequences. She didn't want to upset him any more than she already had.

"It's okay, it's nothing."

"You sure? Well then, I'll be off," Sasai said and hurried into the staff room.

I'm Yuzuru Sasai, age thirty-three.

The owner of the library is my aunt.

My parents both died when I was in first grade in elementary school, in a traffic accident.

My grandparents on my father's side took me in. At the time both sets of my grandparents battled over custody of me. Both wanted to raise me and wouldn't back down, and they ended up going to court. In the end my father's side prevailed, and along with the assets I inherited from my parents, I was sent to live with them.

I heard this only later, but my maternal grandparents basically agreed that my paternal grandparents would have custody, and that I would live with them. In turn, they were asking that they be able to see me more than once a month, and that I could spend long vacations with them. But my paternal grandparents were dead set against this, saying, "We're not going to hand over our eldest son's son." They refused to even let them see me, and after all sorts of misunderstandings it got very heated and the whole thing went south.

My paternal grandparents had fought that hard to have custody, yet once I hit adolescence they found they were too old to handle me, and made me attend a combined junior and senior high school where all the students had to live in the dorms. This school was in the mountains, and was well-known as a place where "problem children" were rehabilitated. It was really more of a reform school or prison. The kind of place that decent parents would never think of putting their child in. I wasn't particularly a delinquent, but was basically forced into the school by my grandparents who didn't know its reputation. Teachers beating the students, students bullying other students—it was all part of daily life there, and it was a living hell.

Around the time I started going to that school, my paternal grandparents both passed away. We weren't in touch anymore with my maternal grandparents. There was no one who could take me in, and all I got was a notice that the money left by my parents would cover my school and dorm fees.

In the fall of my junior year in high school, I was called to the principal's office. This principal, who only seemed to come alive lashing out at students at the morning assembly, was rubbing his hands together and smiling.

"This is Mr. Makoto Sunagawa, a lawyer, who has come here at the request of your relatives."

This lawyer turned to look at me. There was a coffee cup on his table, but it obviously hadn't been touched. When he saw me, he stood up right away. He was nearly six feet tall, broad-chested. Even I, a high school student, could tell at a glance that the suit he wore was a higher quality than that of the principal or other teachers (who mostly wore sweaters anyway).

"You're Yuzuru Sasai?" he asked.

"I am."

He turned to the principal. "Could you please leave us? The two of us need to talk."

"Uh . . . but . . ."

The principal was so startled by this he stared at him.

"But . . . he's still a minor and everything . . ."

"I did show you, didn't I, the document showing I'm representing his legal guardian?"

The lawyer sounded like he was explaining things to someone who wasn't the sharpest pencil in the box.

"You did."

"I told you that was official, correct? You understand my client has legal parental rights?"

"Well, I suppose . . ."

Even so, the principal squirmed a bit and didn't leave, but the lawyer, Mr. Sunagawa, continued to gaze at him, so eventually he gave up and left the room. In other words, the principal left the principal's office.

"Why don't you sit down."

He didn't hesitate to point me toward the seat the principal had just occupied, like this was his own office. I sat down without a word.

"As I just explained, after your grandfather and grandmother passed away, legal parental rights for you have gone to a distant relative. We searched for and located this relative, and the person who retained me has gone through the formal steps to be granted parental rights."

"Is that so."

"My client has a message for you. For these reasons they couldn't come to get you after your grandfather and grandmother passed away, and they want to apologize to you for that."

"I see."

"But now that they have official parental rights, they would like to take you in."

". . . I see," I repeated, and then looked at him in silence.

This continued for a while, and then he laughed. "Isn't there anything you'd like to ask?"

"Like what, for instance?"

"Like who is the client? Or, what kind of person they are? Things like that."

"Who is the client?" I chose to ask.

"For the present I can't say."

Then don't make me ask! I thought.

"If you'd like, you can leave here now and go with me to that person's home. I guarantee it's better than here, and that you can get the kind of education you actually want. If you don't wish to receive an education or don't get along with that person, when you turn twenty and are officially an adult, you'll be free to do whatever you want."

"I see."

"So what do you think?" he asked cheerfully. "You'll go?"

I tilted my head, unsure what to do.

"Simply put, this place is a hell on earth, wouldn't you say?" he said.

"How do you know that?"

"I looked it up online. Graduates of this school have posted some scathing reviews."

"Doesn't surprise me."

"I don't understand why you'd hesitate. Any place you go will be better than here."

"But I don't know if you're really a lawyer. Maybe you're the boss of some human trafficking ring and your client is a pedophile."

We could hardly ever watch TV here, but I'd inherited an old tablet an upperclassman had handed down that eventually made its way to me, and I could log on through a weak Wi-Fi signal from a nearby love hotel. That's how I got to see videos about various urban legends.

I added, "Or your client may not be a pedophiliac, but maybe a person interested in young boys?"

"It's such a nice day out, and . . ." the lawyer said and looked outside. And the weather was good, students in jerseys practicing under a clear blue sky. ". . . our time is limited. I don't want to waste it talking about pedophilia with you . . . Plus, I guess I have to show you this."

So saying, he took out his cell phone, looked up something, and showed me a video online. The video showed a foreigner being jostled by a scrum of reporters and Sunagawa, like he was protecting him, hustling him into a car.

"Do you know this person? He's the president of Japan Electric."

He gave the name of the famous foreign president of the Japanese firm who'd been arrested on suspicion of tax evasion a while ago.

"I'm his lawyer. In Japan I'm quite well-known."

"Hmm."

"I choose my clients carefully. I'm known for only taking on cases when it's worth my while."

"If not money, then what motivates you?"

"This," he said and tapped his heart. "It has to be a case that's good for me to take, one that'll help me grow."

"Is the case of the Japan Electric president being accused of massive tax evasion one that will help you grow?"

"Well, there's a lot more involved in that. The point is—people trust me, and I'm not about to hand you over to someone I don't believe in, someone I don't trust."

"Alright."

"Meaning what?"

"I'll go with you."

"That's pretty sudden."

"I'm telling you—nowhere else could be worse than here."

Sunagawa laughed once more.

LESS THAN A HALF hour after this I was with him, heading for Narita Airport. Just myself, with no baggage. Once I'd agreed to go, the lawyer immediately had the principal come back in.

FINAL EPISODE

"The two of us will be leaving now. Please gather his belongings and send them to my law office."

Both myself and the principal gasped in surprise at his brazenness.

"I mean, you don't have all that many belongings, I would imagine." Sunagawa spoke briskly, like one used to giving orders. "Then let's be off. I have a car waiting for us."

"But . . . we're still in the middle of the second semester, and the other students will be so surprised—No, I mean sad," the flustered principal said.

Sunagawa looked over at me. "Is there anyone you'd like to say goodbye to?"

I shook my head. My class was very wild (actually the whole school was) with kids trembling over who would be the next object of bullying, everyone constantly on edge. I didn't have a single good friend.

"Well then, mark down young Sasai here as quitting school. I'm fine with that."

Sunagawa turned his back on the still-sputtering principal and quickly escorted me to the car, which wasn't a taxi, but a nice shiny black sedan.

Inside the car he continued his explanation.

"Maybe I shouldn't say this, but my client sacrificed a lot, as well as spent a lot of money, in tracing your whereabouts and obtaining parental rights. It took lots of time, with many favors called in and risks involved."

"Did it really cost all that much? Just for me?"

"It did. Like that much," he said, pointing to a condo along the road. "As much as one of those expensive condos."

"Does that include the money paid to you?"

"Yep," he said, nodding, and smiled wryly.

"So what's your point?"

"Nothing really. The client wouldn't tell you this, so I just thought I'd let you know."

At this point the tension started to build in me. I had no idea if I'd be able to be worth all that money, or else leave my benefactor disappointed.

Three hours later we were at Narita Airport and he took me to a private room in a Japanese restaurant in a nearby hotel. When Sunagawa opened the door, a woman was standing by the window, gazing outside. From there you could see all the planes taking off and landing at Narita.

"I've brought him," he announced.

The woman turned around. She was in her mid-fifties and looked remarkably like my mother.

"It's been a long time," she said. "Do you remember me?"

As she said this, I started to tear up a little. I think I

was worried. I didn't understand—why they'd hide the fact that the one who wanted to take care of me was my *aunt*? If they'd only told me, I wouldn't have been so uneasy when I got into the car.

My aunt was my mother's older sister, twelve years older than her. Until my parents died, I only saw her about once a year. I'd heard that she was single and lived in Tokyo. Every time I met her, she bought me whatever I wanted. The last time I saw her was at my parents' funeral.

"But why?" I asked.

This *why* included a lot of things.

Why didn't they tell me it was my aunt? Why did she show up now? Why? *Why?*

My aunt, though, studied me, head tilted, and turned to Sunagawa.

"Are these his only clothes?" she said.

Sunagawa nodded. I had on my school uniform, a white short-sleeve shirt and black trousers.

"Then would you buy him something appropriate, at a shop in the airport, or at the hotel? He can't go to Singapore dressed like this. Jeans and T-shirts should do it. And a few pairs of underwear."

We're going to Singapore?

I was too surprised to say anything. My tears dried up, too.

Sunagawa frowned. "I've never run errands like that before. I am, after all, the best-known lawyer in Japan."

"Then have one of your young staff members handle it."

"None of them are here, unfortunately. I wanted to limit the number of people involved in this case."

"Then please take care of it yourself. I need to talk to the boy."

My aunt opened her dark red leather handbag that was on the table, took out a purse, and casually handed Sunagawa some bills. Left with no other choice, he asked me my clothes sizes and exited the room.

"I'm sorry about that."

After he left her haughty demeanor vanished and she openly apologized.

"I'm sure you were very surprised to see me after all this time. There are all kinds of reasons for it I can't go over right now. I'll explain it all later. As I mentioned, you'll be going to Singapore today."

"Why?"

"Because that's where I live now."

"In Singapore?"

"It's a pretty nice place. It's safe, the food is delicious, and it's laid-back."

". . . But what am I supposed to do in Singapore?"

"Whatever you want. Find a school or something to do there. It's if alright with you."

"But I can't speak English."

"That's okay. I'm not that good at it, either."

"Eh?"

"What do you think? About high school?"

"That's kind of sudden."

"True enough. Just take your time in Singapore and think about school before going back."

"But what about the second semester?"

"Taking a year or two off won't affect your life."

After some time, Sunagawa had returned, and they had me change into the jeans and a T-shirt he brought. Then they handed me the airline ticket and passport they'd arranged, and we set off.

SINGAPORE WAS REALLY A nice place, just like my aunt had said.

My aunt lived in a service apartment in a hotel, the kind with its own kitchen, on Orchard Road, Singapore's main shopping district. I spent my days visiting the zoo and botanical gardens, helping out at a cafe run by a Japanese friend of hers, and attending the occasional class at an English conversation school. They couldn't pay me at the cafe since my visa didn't allow me to work. They did provide lunch, though, and let me take home some high-end coffee beans.

Noticing I wasn't inclined to go to school, my aunt took me to the Kinokuniya Japanese bookstore in Singapore and bought me a ton of Japanese books.

"You can learn most things by reading," she told me. "If you're not going to attend school, I'd like you to read one book per week and then tell me about it when we have dinner on Sundays."

My aunt loved books. Whenever she had free time she was reading, and with books, at least, she'd buy any that I liked.

A few days later she noticed I'd hardly picked up a single one.

"Why don't you read any?" she asked, puzzled by my lack of interest.

"They're boring."

"What kind of books have you read before?"

I was stuck for an answer.

"It doesn't matter which ones, just list a couple."

I still couldn't name a single one.

"Then how about novels? Have you read any stories?"

"*Run, Melos*," I answered.

"That's in high school textbooks, isn't it?"

"*The Restaurant of Many Orders.*"

"Again, something in textbooks."

Now, my aunt gave the title of a few books. "How about *Tom's Midnight Garden*? *Fabre's Book of Insects*? *Anne of Green Gables*? *The Adventures of Sherlock Holmes*? How about *any* Sherlock Holmes books?"

After a moment my aunt let out a sigh.

"You've never read books? It's not something you regularly do?"

"I guess not. When I was in first grade, after my parents were gone, nobody ever made me read."

That evening, after dinner, my aunt and I sat down on the sofa and spent an hour reading. But I just couldn't enjoy it. I couldn't focus on the story and didn't derive any pleasure from it. I'd soon get distracted, look up from my book, and gaze vacantly around the room.

Seeing this, my aunt kept me seated on the sofa and switched to reading aloud to me.

The first book was *My Father's Dragon*. She read only the opening section, where a cat talks to Elmer and he goes on board a boat, then shut the book.

"And *then* what?" I couldn't help but ask.

"What do you mean?"

"Where did Elmer go on the boat? No one discovered him?"

My aunt read a little more of the story.

This quickly became our schedule, her reading aloud

to me for an hour before bedtime. And I finally came to enjoy books.

I had to know what happened next. Was Elmer able to meet the dragon? Was he able to run away through the jungle and not get snagged by some fearsome animal?

A few days later, during the afternoon when my aunt was out, I picked up the book and read on myself. After I finished the whole Elmer series, I moved on to *The Adventures of Sherlock Holmes*, and started reading contemporary Japanese novels.

I had finally become a reader.

ONE MORNING, ABOUT THREE months after we came to Singapore, my aunt asked, as she gazed at her computer screen, "Why don't we go to Europe next? Italy or somewhere?"

"Italy?"

"Paris is good too."

I was brewing some coffee then. I wasn't a big coffee fan, but I'd learned how to make it at the cafe. My aunt told me my coffee was delicious, and that became the only task I had to do around the home.

Truthfully, I had no desire to go to Europe. I loved the southern air of Singapore, and there was a Japanese girl I'd grown fond of who was also working part-time at the cafe. She helped me with my English, and on days off showed me around places like Katong and Bugis.

"I thought if you were going to attend high school we could stay here for a while," my aunt told me, seriously, "but if not, I'd like to leave. I'm sure you'll love Europe," she added. "If we go to Italy we should stay in a hotel or guesthouse run by farmers. The food will be delicious."

"We'll come back here again next year," she said, and I reluctantly agreed.

And Italy was amazing, too, just like she said. I helped out, again unpaid, in a vineyard, studied Italian a bit in a school, and some farmers taught me how to drive a car.

My aunt was much better at Italian than English, and she taught me as well. Apparently when she was young, she studied for a while at an art school in Italy.

Three months into our stay she said, "How about we go to Cambodia next? Let's study history and art at Angkor Wat."

And as I traveled the world with her, I came to realize that my aunt was one of those people who were *eternal travelers*. In most countries if you stayed more than six months you were obligated to start paying taxes. She was a person who turned this system around, staying in countries where you can stay for a handful of months without a visa, and as long as you don't own a house or have a set address, you legally do not have to pay any taxes at all.

However, from around the time my aunt and I met, a system was taking shape throughout the world to make it obligatory that these *eternal travelers* be taxed. Enforcement was getting stricter, with the possibility that they would have a tax liability back in Japan. Because of this, my aunt did her utmost to enter and leave Japan without anyone knowing and could only let the minimum number of people know her location at any time.

"But if you said you wanted to go to high school," she told me, "I was thinking of settling down there. It's true."

My aunt said this as she was explaining her lifestyle to me.

"But I know you never seemed to want to go to high school," she added.

"And you took advantage of that?"

"Ha-ha! You got me!"

But the truth only came out later, at an unexpected time.

For several years, I went all over the world with

my aunt. We traveled to Hawaii and Paris, in Thailand and India. In London we stayed for a long time in a five-star hotel that had been featured in movies, and at a ¥1,000/night dorm in Malacca. Most of the time, though, we stayed in her friends' villas or in people's guesthouses.

Before I realized it, my English had improved by leaps and bounds and I was the one who proposed the next place we should visit.

The turning point came just before I turned twenty. One morning I suddenly found I couldn't get out of bed.

"I think the exhaustion of all our trips has caught up with you," my aunt said.

We were living on the island of Hawaii at the time.

My aunt called the coffee plantation I was helping at, telling them I was taking a day off. Even now, I remember clearly hearing her happily tell them on the phone, as I lay in bed, that "Yuzu's not feeling well. In Japanese we say it's like the devil gets sunstroke, since a strong boy like him rarely gets sick."

But the next day, too, I couldn't drag myself out of bed. Or the next day, or the day after that.

"What could be wrong, I wonder?" my aunt said. "Should I take you to a hospital?"

She hadn't been worried at all at first, but gradually her face grew pale.

I didn't have a fever and wasn't coughing. But my body felt listless, and I just couldn't get up. It felt like a long bout of seasickness. The year before we'd spent a month on a high-end cruise ship, so I knew what seasickness felt like.

I didn't feel nauseated or dizzy, either. But it did feel like that hopeless bad feeling when you can't manage to get off the ship. Mental seasickness, perhaps.

We borrowed a neighbor's car and drove to a general hospital on the island. The diagnosis didn't take long—a mild case of depression.

"What should we do?" My aunt, up till then calm and collected, now sounded flustered.

"It'll get better if I sleep. And they gave me medicine for it, too." I was the calm one now.

But things didn't go that well. For another month I barely left my room.

My aunt took me to Oahu, to the biggest and most reputable hospital there where they examined me.

The upshot was I had a long period of rest and recovery. We found a good, Japanese-speaking psychiatrist and psychoanalyst. My illness was caused by all the trauma in my childhood—losing my parents when I was in first grade, relatives fighting over custody, being sent to that school where I was on edge every single minute.

"Am I to blame?" my aunt said, weeping a little. "Dragging you all over the world like that."

"I don't think so. Even though I got sick, it was fun, and I didn't mind at all," I said.

"But *I* mind."

"Okay, but isn't it about time we have to leave the US?"

My *eternal traveler* aunt's period of stay was almost up.

"You don't need to worry about that," she said when I asked this. "Living with you, I've come to understand—that you're the most precious thing in the world to me. So just don't worry. I'm not good at paperwork and things, and I'll leave the difficult things up to Mr. Sunagawa."

"But all that costs money, doesn't it?"

"Nothing's easier than solving things using money."

My aunt contacted many relevant places so we could stay in Hawaii longer. It must have been a lot of trouble for her—there were taxes involved, of course, money for visas and hospital visits, and the not inconsiderable expenses for all the counseling sessions. But she spent all her money and time to make sure I got the treatment I needed.

My aunt went for counseling, too. The psychoanalyst requested we do that. His diagnosis was that this illness wasn't my problem alone but was connected with long-term issues within our family. She accepted that, and apparently had her own appointments with this psychoanalyst, apart from my sessions.

A year passed and I was able to walk around outside as usual. Once I was able to go outside, we went to have breakfast together at the Halekulani Hotel. As we enjoyed the ocean view my aunt said, "You are, for sure, the greatest gift my younger sister ever gave me."

"You think?"

"Thanks to you I've gotten better mentally, too."

Even after our treatment finished, we remained in Oahu for a while. She seemed anxious that if we changed venues it might spark a relapse. One morning, as I was brewing coffee, I said, "I think I would like to go to school . . . and study in college if I can."

A smile gradually spread over my aunt's whole face.

"That's wonderful," she said.

I got the feeling she'd been waiting for me to say something like that.

"And also . . ."

Telling her this next part took more courage than my decision to go to college.

"I want to be your child. I want us to be a family." When I turned twenty and became an adult, my aunt lost her parental rights over me. I wanted her to adopt me.

She shook her head.

"I appreciate that, I do. But you need to carry on your father's last name—Sasai. I think my sister and he would have wanted that. Plus, we're already like a parent and child, aren't we?"

My aunt wouldn't concede. So though I didn't become her actual adopted son, I thought of her as my parent, and continued to act that way. That was the one point *I* didn't concede.

I went back to Japan by myself, took the high school equivalency exam, went to the Philippines to brush up on my English, then attended a college in America. My aunt, of course, paid for the tuition.

This brought my world tour with my aunt to a close. She went off on trips by herself now. And we never lived together again. She continued her one-woman travels as before, and we occasionally got in touch. Five years ago, though, she announced that she was "coming back to Japan."

Shortly before this, the regulations governing these *eternal travelers* like her had gotten stricter. No longer could she go without paying any taxes.

"The tax thing is part of it," she said, "but frankly I'm tired of traveling. I want to live in a place where I can wear *geta* while slurping down some soba noodles in Japan in one of those little stands where you eat standing up. Plus, I've found something I'd like to try to do."

By that time I had graduated from college and was working at an IT-related company in Tokyo.

What my aunt wanted to try was to create the Night Library. Through all of her studies of art, she'd discovered the importance of preserving this thing known as the *past*.

"You know, it's presumptuous to think that the present is more advanced than the past," she said. "Putting aside industry, science, and chemistry, there hasn't been any progress in the arts, or literature."

She told me this while she stood in front of the statue *David* in the Accademia Gallery.

"Probably we can't produce magnificent things like this nowadays. Apart from reproductions and such."

"Hmm."

"Which is why I'd like to take the past and seal it in."

After I heard her plans for the Night Library, my immediate response was, "Would you let me help you with it?"

Something about what she said struck me. I had a vague sense of why my aunt was willing to stake her life on this. And I also felt like this was a way of repaying her for all she'd done for me.

When she heard my reply, she nodded. A smile spread, ever so slowly, across her face, from the center to the sides.

I think she knew that's what I was going to say.

"Have you decided where you're going during your time off?"

Otoha asked this during the second time the library was closed, right after they'd watched *Anne of Green Gables*. Minami darted a glance at Masako and Ako. Not intentionally, she thought, but Masako kept her eyes down, while Ako looked away.

"I'm thinking of having my parents come see me . . ." Otoha said.

Not particularly interested in the others' plans, Otoha went on, unconcerned about their reactions. Honestly, she'd broached the subject because she wanted them to listen to what she was going to say.

"My, that sounds quite nice," Masako said, raising her head. "Have you already invited them to come?"

Otoha nodded as she reached out for a slice of the pizza that Ako had baked for them. Recently, whenever they gathered, Ako always cooked dishes sure to please young women—curry, pizza, quiche.

"My parents work too, so Saturday's the only time they can visit."

"Have you decided where you'll take them?"

"That's the problem. I asked them where they'd like to go but they said anywhere's fine. Which isn't helpful . . . Ueno Zoo, Tokyo Tower, Roppongi Hills are all so far from here. If all they see are the mountains and fields around here it'll just disappoint them since they're no different from back home."

"I think they're saying that as long as they can be with you, *anywhere*, as they said, is fine with them." Ako smiled as she said this and poured Otoha some iced tea. This, too, was homemade tea she'd prepared. Very fragrant, with a refreshing hint of mint. She was apparently growing peppermint on the tiny veranda of her apartment.

"Parents are like that. If they can see you, and talk with you, that's all they need."

Otoha frowned. "No, my folks aren't that sappy! They let me have it straight when it comes to jobs, and they aren't at all happy with me. I'm going to endure yet another sermon, I'm sure of it."

"I don't think so. All they need to see is the dorm and the library. Aren't they worried about what kind of place you're working at?"

Masako agreed.

But Otoha's parents' opposition to her working there was something she'd already told them about.

"You think so?" Otoha said.

"I do. Have them stay in your room, take them shopping at the stores near the station . . . and if you can, show them around the library, and that should be enough, don't you think?"

"Right. But the library's closed."

"Why don't you borrow the key just that one day . . . ?"

"Is that possible? I'm sure Mr. Sasai's holding on to the keys during the closure."

"He lives just a short bike ride from here, so why don't you go ask him? I'm sure if you talk with him and tell him you'll just keep them half a day, he'll allow it."

"I'll think about it."

Otoha gave a resigned sort of nod, but what Ako and the others were saying was starting to make sense. It had the added plus of not costing a lot. After her parents left, she was thinking of going to Cebu Island in the Philippines for a short-term study program, but had only gathered information and was still up in the air about it.

"If they stay in your room, tell them I'll lend them futon bedding from mine," Masako offered.

"Really? You'll be okay?" Otoha said.

"Yes, I'm planning to go on a trip myself," Masako said.

"Wow. That's great. On your own?" Minami asked loudly, but then looked a bit sullen. She thought it was a harmless question, but noticed she may have overstepped and invaded Masako's privacy.

"That's right." Masako answered cheerfully, as if laughing away the others' concerns. "I'm thinking of going to a hot spring."

"Hot spring. Now that's pretty elegant."

"Nothing elegant about it. It's a small inn deep in the mountains. The room is a tiny tatami room, with a futon and TV and that's it. It used to be used for hot spring cures and there's a communal kitchen where you can cook for yourself. Overnight without meals it's less than ¥5,000."

"There used to be a lot of inns like that in the old days." Ako nodded.

"Cooking's too much trouble for me so I'll have them provide some simple meals. They say it's hard to get internet or cell phone service out there."

"Really? What're you going to do in a place like that?" Otoha blurted out.

"Read as much as I like, of course. I'm going to bring along books I haven't read yet and finish them all."

Various comments arose: *That's wonderful! How charming! Classic Masako!* Masako watched all this, a faint smile on her face. When all the words of praise had died down, she murmured, "And then I'll make sure of something."

"Make sure of what?" Otoha asked.

But Masako didn't explain any more.

FINAL EPISODE

"It's a secret," she said, leaving a smile behind.

"What about you, Ako?" Minami asked.

"I'm thinking I'll sell my house."

"What?" Otoha and Minami said in surprise. Masako didn't say anything, though she did stare intently at Ako.

"I've been trying to decide what to do about it for a long time. A house in the country . . . actually a shop, a tiny, tiny bookshop. With the rise of online stores, the sales of books there went way down, and it's been closed for a long time, but I just haven't been up to selling it or taking care of all the things inside."

"You're okay selling it?" Masako gazed into Ako's face.

"Yeah. I decided. It's in a 'nothing' kind of place, small and old, but since it's near the roundabout in front of the station there is a buyer. He said he's going to make it into a convenience store. And the offer's not bad. So I think I may . . ." Ako licked her lips. "Even if I divide the profit among my family, there'll be enough to help me in my old age."

"Does your family agree with that?" Otoha asked. She realized she'd never once heard anything about Ako's family.

"What do you think? I don't know. I mean, I don't have any other ideas about what to do with the shop. The only thing that's decided is I'm not going back there again. So I imagine it's okay. Doing that, I think, will be the happiest solution."

Happiest for who? It was unclear, but Otoha hesitated to ask more.

"If you think that's best, Ako, then . . ."

"If I sell it and wire the money to her, I'm sure it will help her out. That bank account's the only connection she and I have at this point." She sounded like she was talking to herself.

"She?" Hearing all this, Otoha couldn't remain indifferent.

"Yeah. My daughter."

"You have a daughter then?"

"Yes. Um. I think she's working in the Kansai area now, probably. She might even be married. I'm happy if she is. I'm not saying I want her to marry, but I'd like it if there's someone she has in her life she can be happy with."

Ako nodded at her own words.

"Are you okay, Ako?" Minami asked worriedly.

"I'm fine. It's my fault my daughter and I don't get along. All my fault. I expected too much of her. My husband died when my daughter was little, and I was always after her, telling her do this, do that. It was too much. I want you to be nearby, I told her, go to a local high school and college. I told her that, as far as a job, she should take over the bookstore, and if possible marry someone willing to legally claim the name of our family and take our last name . . . I didn't intend it to sound so overbearing. I just wanted her to know my wishes. But for my daughter it was a burden. For her, my words were a straitjacket, and before I knew it she'd left home, saying she was going to Tokyo to college. And I haven't seen her since. She's stayed in touch with her cousin so at least I know she's still alive, but that's all. But she said she doesn't want to talk to me."

"So that's what happened . . ."

"The bank account is one I opened for her when she worked part-time at the bookstore, so I could pay her that way. I told her to save it up and use when she got married, so I know the account number. Transferring money to that account is the only connection she and I have now."

The rest of them fell silent.

". . . I'm fine with it. I'm very grateful to be able to go on working here. And I've come to a decision to sell that shop, and let my daughter go."

Ako, perhaps noticing how Minami was looking like she was about to cry, said, "One thing's struck me as I've worked with you, Minami, and with Otoha. How you young people working here are so dedicated, so kind and happy looking. I think my daughter must be the same. So I've decided to make it on my own. Thanks to all of you."

Is that really true? Otoha wondered.

Those was her honest feelings, of course, but wasn't she holding out a faint hope? That sending a large amount of money to her, her daughter would then reach out to her?

Yes, she must be thinking that way. And Otoha felt sorry for Ako, clinging to that slight hope. On the other hand, she also felt like only the two of them could really understand their parent-child relationship. The Ako who got along well with us, Otoha thought, was, to her daughter, a person she hated to be around.

People change, according to who they're with.

". . . I hesitated about whether I should say all this," Minami timidly said. "I was thinking not to tell you."

"Tell us what?" Masako asked. "Some shocking confession?"

This exaggerated expression seemed to be Masako's way of intentionally lightening the heavy atmosphere.

"No, it's not like that . . . Or maybe it is, a little." Minami's voice grew steadily quieter. "During this time off . . . I'm thinking of going for an interview in Tokyo."

"Interview? You mean a job interview?" Otoha asked.

"Right. I wasn't going to mention it."

Minami looked over at Ako.

"After Ako's shocking confession, I felt like I wanted to share."

"What? It's my fault?" Ako was back to her usual carefree ways.

"But why, Minami? You always seem to enjoy it here so much." Otoha's voice was so surprised that she couldn't help speaking loudly.

"It's not like I'm dissatisfied with working here. It's quite the opposite. I enjoy it, and everyone here is so nice . . . But the thing is, I realized maybe I don't really like books all that much. I can't get as excited as all of you do over books or novels. So I think it might be better to let someone else do my job."

"No way."

"I don't think library staff all have to be people who love books and novels," Masako said quietly. "Rather, I think libraries also need people who can judge things calmly."

"Thank you for saying that," Minami said, bowing slightly. "But I was thinking about other workplaces . . . being a regular company employee? Thinking I might try office work. After college I've only worked in libraries, and all I've dealt with are somewhat old books. I feel I'd like to view them more from the outside."

"I see."

This was all quite a shock to Otoha. If Minami left, there would be no one else here her own age. Still, she wanted to support her friend's decision.

"I don't know what's going to happen yet," Minami said. "I mean, I might fail all the interviews. It's entirely possible. I might go for interviews and realize I like it better here after all."

Minami might say that, but to Otoha it seemed like she'd already made up her mind.

When she got back to her room, Otoha suddenly remembered.

She'd totally forgotten to say anything about Saho Oda or *Koko Kobayashi*.

IT WAS DURING MY recovery time on Oahu that my aunt revealed the source of her wealth.

When she was young, she studied art in Bologna, Italy, and before she entered college she'd attended a local language school for a time. There were people from all different countries there, including a group from an Arab country.

Rumor had it that one man was the relative of the king, the others his followers-cum-bodyguards. They always did things together as a group, five or six of them.

The group was overbearing, strolling around the language school like they owned the place. Everyone especially hated the boss, the relative of the king. He'd look around the classroom and says things like, "I use more money in a year than all these people will ever earn in their lifetimes," and "I'm going to study Italian and bring home an Italian woman as my fourth wife." Even the teacher hated him, and would intentionally have him repeat, over and over, words that were hard for him to pronounce.

One day, though, my aunt spotted one of the group in the cafeteria who seemed to be having trouble, and she helped out.

"His credit card had been declined and he couldn't pay for his meal, so I lent him some cash. Everybody saw he was having problems, but they hated him so much they pretended not to notice, and no one stepped in to help."

My aunt had already gathered that the man was the youngest among the Arab group, and the quietest. He was the only one who, when given the cold shoulder in class, looked sad about it.

To thank my aunt for helping him, he invited her out to dinner. Minus any of the others in his clique, of course. His Italian was poor, but he spoke beautiful English. When he was a child, he told her, he attended school in England. In times between his protection detail for the royal family he invited my aunt out. During the several months of the language school curriculum, he and my aunt began dating.

At the time my aunt was already thirty, having graduated from college and worked several years as a regular company employee before she came to study abroad there in Italy. He was much younger, having only just graduated from a college back home.

"Japanese look young for their age and it seems he didn't notice the age difference," Sasai's aunt said.

On the day the language school program was over, he proposed to her. And surprisingly, he confessed that the king's relative wasn't that obnoxious man in their party but he himself. Going abroad like this to study was part of a trip he was given to celebrate his graduation from college, and after he returned he was to assume a high-level role in the government.

"Imagine my surprise. His pretending to be one of the security guards was all a ruse for his protection. If people knew he was in the royal family their attitudes would change, and he wanted to be with all kinds of people without that framing the interaction. Once he began his post, he would hardly ever be able to leave his country."

My aunt didn't dislike him, Sasai recalled, but she turned him down. Her plan was to study in an Italian college after this, and she didn't like the idea of becoming his second wife. (He was already married, his first wife betrothed to him since they were children.) Also, his entourage had reported back to their country about my aunt, and his parents were dead set against it. Which was understandable, considering he wanted to bring a much older Japanese back with him.

He was sad about it, but there was nothing he could do. He returned to his country and my aunt remained in Italy.

He rarely went abroad after this, but my aunt went to see him often. Each time, he gave her an *allowance*. Like she was his mistress, which my aunt wasn't happy about. He told her, a sad look on his face, that the money was a paltry amount and he had nothing else he could give her, so she had to accept. He seemed to feel very apologetic to her and felt responsible since he'd made the proposal and it was his parents who'd refused to accept it.

During the time she went to see him, he added another wife, then another, to his family. In his world these were unavoidable political marriages of convenience. My aunt couldn't figure out if these were truly necessary, or if he was simply a womanizer. Yet each time he added another wife, he presented my aunt with a large amount of money.

When his wife count reached three, he proposed to my aunt once again. He was thirty, my aunt within shouting distance of forty. If they didn't marry now, he said, he couldn't have any more wives, so this was their last chance to marry. He was already the head of a large family, with eight children.

"I didn't feel like waltzing into a situation like that, and if I had, I probably would never be able to leave his country."

Religion, too, was an issue. If they married she would have to convert, wear a head-to-foot outfit and live a cloistered life in her house, in a country where she knew hardly anyone. My aunt wasn't particularly opposed to Islam, yet she didn't believe in the existence of God in any form. She was an atheist.

Once again my aunt turned down his proposal.

Finally, when he took his fourth wife, he once again gave my aunt a huge amount of money, enough for her to live on comfortably for the rest of her life. Also, since he held an important post in finance in his country, he was well versed in investments and taught my aunt the information needed to invest and become an eternal traveler.

Around this time, their relationship seemed to have ended.

He climbed the ladder of success, becoming a minister in the government and scion of a large family, and was extremely busy. Casually meeting some unexplained Oriental woman became more and more impossible.

For her part, my aunt got used to traveling here and there around the world. And over ten years passed without her and the man actually meeting face-to-face, though they stayed in touch.

Even now, he has her on retainer as an adviser and occasionally they'll speak on Skype. She must receive quite a bit of money for this as well. Further, he was the first financial supporter of this Night Library. I think he still loves my aunt and depends on her for emotional support.

When thefts at the library started to occur frequently, and an odd person appeared, it was this man who worried about my aunt and dispatched Mr. Kuroiwa to work there. He apparently asked a Japanese security company to find an appropriate former police officer for the job. He was also the one who hired Mr. Sunagawa, the lawyer, to be her go-to legal adviser.

She found this library, unused, in the outskirts of Tokyo and gradually remodeled it, but the older real estate agent who was the go-between began stalking her in a way, and she grew terrified. Every time she was exposed to people's malice and persistence it exhausted her.

On top of that, my aunt grew old.

When I got to know her, I thought she was kind of odd because she had become very obstinate, and basically had cut all ties with other people. She tended to be that way from the beginning but as she got older and went through hardships this became more pronounced.

I was the only person she would talk with face-to-face.

After a Skype interview with library staff candidates, she'd take to her bed for days. "Talking to other people leaves me exhausted," she told me. "Their raw emotions and words aren't bad, but being overwhelmed by them is hard for me."

My view is she's overly considerate.

After she speaks to these people, she mutters to herself for a while. Says things like *I should have said this, I should have reacted to that, My response might have hurt their feelings* . . . verbalizing her feelings of regret.

The only way for her to recover is to take to her bed for a few days, waiting for the memories to fade.

I asked her once what criteria she used when she hired people.

"I choose those who are hurt, and exhausted," she answered right away.

I couldn't help but smile. Since I thought wanting to help people who suffered in some way when dealing with books was a wonderful reason. When I heard what she said next, though, my smile retreated.

"And people who have secrets. Put those to good

use, use their weaknesses to make them at my beck and call."

"Why would you do that?"

"People change. You don't know what's going to happen next. If something does happen, I want to be able to deal with it. To protect you, and this place."

My aunt was certainly not just some kind, charitable person. I knew this from a long time ago, but her words now only reinforced it.

At the time I thought this. Just as my aunt protected me, would I be able to protect this library, my aunt, and the people who worked here—all of them? It wouldn't be easy, but I knew I had to make it happen.

Up till then, she was never on the front lines of the library and was happy just cleaning the building and the dorm. She never spoke with any of the staff, though she was occasionally proud that she knew them better than anyone.

"Talk with a person about the books they read, and you can tell what sort of person they are."

"I don't know about that."

I really wasn't sure.

"Then you take a look at their bookshelves. A person's desires are crammed into their bookshelf. Look at that and you can tell what kind of person they want to become."

She had a master key to the dorm rooms. Which made sense, since she cleaned the dorm and was, in actual fact, the landlord. From time to time she would apparently enter their rooms and study their bookshelves . . . which may have accounted for earlier ghostly feelings on the part of at least one resident.

"I don't do anything bad. Just check out their bookshelves, that's all."

It worried me how my aunt was retreating more into her shell and growing more eccentric. I knew I'd have to keep a sharp eye out.

Maybe she loved that man more than she realized, and was tormenting herself because of the fate that kept them apart, and her regret at the decision she made back then.

If I asked her about it, though, I suppose she would deny it.

The man had written two books. One was specialized, published in his own name, about his country's economy. The second was one he secretly published, in English, in the UK under a pen name. A novel, a love story.

And this was one more reason my aunt created this library.

In order to keep his collection, as a novelist, always near her.

FINAL EPISODE

In the past she'd spent many hours in his own personal library in his home. Sometimes alone, sometimes the two of them. His romance novel was born there, with my aunt giving advice. His will specified that after his death, his collection would be donated to a certain Japanese *library*. It wasn't possible to just give it to some unknown Asian woman as the recipient—which would raise too many questions.

It was my aunt's desires that made this into the "Night Library."

At first when I asked why it would only be open at night, she said, "The daylight will damage these precious books," and "The time difference between Japan and his country is six hours ahead and he gets in touch very late, so it's best to be up and about at night." Yet the real reason was that during the off hours, she used the library herself then.

During the day she was the true owner of the library. She simply steeped herself in the books and words and spent time reading.

Since she invested her personal assets in the library, I think she could be allowed this little indulgence.

The incident with Kimiko Ninomiya, though, completely wore her out.

"I want to close the library for a while," she said, greatly troubled when I updated her on what was happening.

"How long is *for a while*?" I asked.

My voice was trembling. Just as Otoha Higuchi was starting to sense, I got the feeling the library would never open again.

"For a while means just that, for a while."

My aunt frowned and didn't elaborate.

Like the library, my aunt closed up as well.

During this time off, I needed somehow to get her to open up again.

That's, frankly, all I can think about right now. I have to protect this library from closing, and my aunt from closing herself off.

The moth specimen at the entrance to the library was a present from that man. He donated funds to all sorts of universities and foundations, and that included his research into insects, and he was asked to name a new species of moth.

My aunt's name is Koko Kobayashi. *Koko* is written with characters meaning *child of the rainbow*.

THE COLLECTION INVENTORY WAS nearly finished two days before the closure began. Fortunately, there were no missing books, and only two were found without collection stamps (thought to be the handiwork of Kimiko Ninomiya).

FINAL EPISODE

On the last day they cleaned the library and made all the preparations for when they would welcome patrons back.

Otoha and Masako and Ako, the collections sorting team, moved all the books in the collections of Tadasuke Shirakawa and Mizuki Takashiro from the conference room to the sorting room. After the library reopened, sorting these would be their first job. Other staff members who were free helped them move all the boxes.

"Mr. Kinoshita is in the dining hall, you know," Minami whispered to Otoha as they used a dolly to transport the books.

"Really?!"

"He said he'll make a midnight meal for us."

Otoha suddenly felt energized.

After they'd moved all the books, Otoha excused herself to Masako and the others and headed to the dining hall. The lights really were on, and Mr. Kinoshita was busy behind the counter.

"How have you been, Mr. Kinoshita? It's been a while."

"Yeah," he answered simply. Embarrassed, perhaps, or perhaps finding it too much trouble to say more, he confined himself to a small nod.

"Are you serving something today?"

"Um. Sit down and I'll be with you."

After talking with Minami and Tokuda, Mr. Kinoshita came over, wearing his apron.

"I actually didn't feel like coming, but I thought it must be the final day of the inventory, so I wanted to make something for you all."

"I'm grateful," Otoha said, bowing deeply. "So what are you serving today?"

"When I realized this, it was already night, and though I don't have much here, I could use the canned goods I've stored away if that's okay."

"Of course."

"I hurriedly turned on the rice cooker a little while ago. It'll take a while to cook. Ten minutes, maybe."

"How many more can you feed, Mr. Kinoshita?"

"I cooked plenty of rice, and have a lot of canned goods, so as many as want to can eat."

"So can I go tell others to come?"

"Yeah, sure. And I have a stock of microbrewery beer, so you guys can celebrate the end of your inventory."

"Yay!"

Otoha and Minami ran downstairs and told Sasai, Masako, and the others. Ms. Kitazato at the reception desk, too, of course.

"Is it okay if I go too?" she asked. "I've hardly ever eaten there before . . ."

Ako and the others looked a bit apologetic, but happy nonetheless.

FINAL EPISODE

By the time Otoha and Minami returned to the dining hall the food was ready and laid out on their table.

"This really is just something I threw together with the canned goods I had on hand. So don't expect much," Kinoshita said.

In a donburi bowl, on top of the rice, were four or five little fish, and a scattering of sliced scallions. Accompanying this was soup in lacquered bowls.

"And this would be . . . ?"

"Try it first."

Otoha picked up the donburi bowl and put one of the small fish and rice into her mouth.

"It's delicious, Mr. Kinoshita. It looks so very simple, but it's amazing."

"I just warmed up canned oil sardines in a frying pan, added some soy sauce, and put it and the sardine oil over rice. That's it. The scallions I bought at a convenience store on the way here 'cause it was the only place open. But it works, doesn't it?"

"It does. I could eat a ton of this rice."

"It's a recipe in an essay by the novelist Yoko Mori. The soup is an egg soup with dried wakame seaweed and eggs."

As Otoha and the others dug in, the rest of the staff who'd come to the library that day showed up.

Mr. Kinoshita asked them all how hungry they were, and any particular likes and dislikes, and served them oil sardine donburi bowls in turn. And brought out some small bottles of the microbrew beer.

"It's like a little celebration," Minami whispered to Otoha.

"It really is. Hey . . . Minami."

"Mmm?"

Minami, beer bottle to her lips as she took a drink, looked over at Otoha. Wanting to lessen the numbers of dishes for Kinoshita to wash they all opted to drink their beer straight from the bottle.

"Please don't tell me you're going to quit, it's too sad." Otoha said this quietly so as not to be overheard. "This is fun, isn't it? I doubt you can do this at any other company."

". . . Well, I'll check out all kinds of places and think about it."

Think about it—everything seemed to be wrapped up in those words.

This week Minami would probably be going for interviews, visiting companies, and seriously considering her next move. Whatever the answers were that she got, Otoha and the others wouldn't be able to deny or stop her.

Masako and Ako were seated a little way off, eating, and Mr. Kinoshita was talking with them. The three of them would make a great photo, she thought, and the others too, Tokuda, for instance, intently discussing something with Sasai, and Tokai and Kitazato smiling at each other. They looked so great together, like a real couple, not that that meant they were going out or anything. Though Otoha thought it wouldn't be a bad idea down the road.

Whatever the people here do, she thought, they're free to choose.

What would she and Sasai do, though?

If possible, I want to get nearer to him, she thought, *be with him, hear more of what he has to say. Later I'll go over to him*, she thought. *And talk with him while we eat.*

But even if I can't, this whole atmosphere now is precious, a wonderful time, but not one that will last forever.

Otoha casually left the dining hall. She glanced back to check that no one had noticed her and went down to the first floor.

She looked in the women's bathroom near the reception desk and found Ms. Kobayashi scrubbing the toilet there. She was kneeling on the floor, her face almost inside the bowl, scrubbing away with a cloth. No patrons were coming these days, so Otoha didn't think it could be all that dirty.

As she gazed at the older woman an odd emotion welled up inside her.

"Shall I help you?"

She'd actually been thinking of saying something else, but those were the words that came out.

Ms. Kobayashi slowly turned around. She wore a bandana pulled down over her head and a large mask over her face, so all Otoha could make out was a glimpse of her eyes. She said nothing, merely shaking her head. And turned back to scrubbing the toilet.

"Please. Let me help."

Why hadn't I ever offered before? she wondered.

Otoha took a scrub cloth from the cleaning cart and opened the stall next to the toilet Kobayashi was cleaning. It was a Japanese squatting style toilet, and for an instant she hesitated, but then knelt down even more than Kobayashi and commenced scrubbing.

Kobayashi made no comment.

"Don't close it down," Otoha said, as she stared at the toilet. And again there was no response. Thinking she hadn't heard, Otoha repeated herself.

"I believe you're the library's owner, Ms. Kobayashi . . . This place is so precious to me. Please, don't close it down . . ."

"When you were working at a book store, you caused an incident, didn't you. Before you came here."

This was the first time she'd really heard Kobayashi's voice. It was a stronger voice than she'd imagined, a lovely, young voice. But more than that *what* she said had startled her.

"How do you know that?" Otoha gasped.

"When you were by yourself, a large amount of money went missing from the register, and they said you did it."

"That is simply wrong. I did not do that."

"But that was the reason the store used to fire you. But you never told anyone. Is it okay for me to tell others?"

"Huh?!"

"Can I tell, for instance, your parents, or Sasai? Tell them the truth?"

"No way . . ."

"Then don't butt in when you shouldn't say anything."

Scrub cloth in hand, Otoha walked around behind Kobayashi. And looked at her, scrubbing away.

During the interview, the owner hadn't asked the reason she'd left the bookstore. There was no need, since she already knew.

"I never did that. That's absolutely wrong."

Otoha suspected it was the store manager who had stolen the money. But she had no positive proof, and besides, he had a family. She couldn't make a scene about the false charges.

"If you want to tell on me, Ms. Kobayashi, go ahead. No, I'll tell everyone myself. But *please* keep this library open. I need this place, and so do others. There are some who will have nowhere else to go if this place is no more. And I won't tell anybody you're the owner."

Again, Kobayashi slowly turned around. She gazed long and hard at Otoha, looking her right in the eye.

"You don't need to say that," Kobayashi said.

"Huh?"

"I know you didn't steal that money. I invited you here because I believe you."

Otoha's eyes suddenly teared up.

"You should go. Go back and join the others."

"But . . ."

"Don't worry, I won't do anything to cause trouble for all of you. I'm responsible for asking all of you to work here."

"Really?"

"If I say I'll take responsibility, I will."

". . . I understand."

Otoha put the scrub cloth back on the cart and washed her hands in the sink. It was only then that she realized her cheeks were wet and that she was trembling.

When she got back to the dining hall it was the same as when she had left, everyone eating and talking with each other.

Her eyes met Sasai's as he was talking with Tokuda. Sasai was looking at Otoha as if he was going to ask her something, but Tokuda spoke to him and he turned away.

FINAL EPISODE

Otoha sat down again next to Minami.

"What happened?" Minami asked as she sipped her beer.

"What do you mean?"

"Where did you go? You were gone a long time . . ."

"I went to the bathroom."

Which was true enough.

"Oh."

Unaware of what Otoha had done, and said, the others went on talking and enjoying the meal.

Will this library go on? Will the owner really keep her promise to me?

Otoha shut her eyes. Everyone's voice sounded so far away, perhaps because she was getting a bit tipsy.

I don't know how long this will stay as it is, Otoha thought.

But maybe the fact that it's not forever is exactly what makes it all the more beautiful.

★ ★ ★ ★ ★